Meredith Webber lives on the sunny Gold Coast in Queensland, Australia, but takes regular trips west into the Outback, fossicking for gold or opal. These breaks in the beautiful and sometimes cruel red earth country provide her with an escape from the writing desk and a chance for her mind to roam free—not to mention getting some much needed exercise. They also supply the kernels of so many stories that it's hard for her to stop writing!

We hope you've enjoyed
Conveniently Wed in Paradise
Meredith Webber's 100th book!

Also by Meredith Webber

A Sheikh to Capture Her Heart
Healed by Her Army Doc
New Year Wedding for the Crown Prince
A Wife for the Surgeon Sheikh
The Doctors' Christmas Reunion

The Halliday Family miniseries

A Forever Family for the Army Doc
Engaged to the Doctor Sheikh
A Miracle for the Baby Doctor
From Bachelor to Daddy

Discover more at millsandboon.co.uk.

$

Pl(
Bc

Tele
Ema
Onli
Twit
Face:

___

/

EZ0:

CONVENIENTLY WED IN PARADISE

MEREDITH WEBBER

MILLS & BOON

First published in Great Britain 2020
by Mills & Boon, an imprint of HarperCollins*Publishers*
1 London Bridge Street, London, SE1 9GF

Large Print edition 2020

© 2020 Meredith Webber

ISBN: 978-0-263-08583-9

MIX
Paper from
responsible sources
FSC
www.fsc.org   FSC® C007454

This book is produced from independently certified FSC™ paper to ensure responsible forest management. For more information visit www.harpercollins.co.uk/green.

Printed and bound in Great Britain
by CPI Group (UK) Ltd, Croydon, CR0 4YY

Thanks to all my family,
who've suffered along the way,
and to the writing friends
I've made in the angst-ridden,
neurotic, wonderful world of writing.

And special thanks to
Elizabeth Johnson, who accepted my
first book and gave me the strength
and encouragement to write another,
and another, and…

CHAPTER ONE

ALEXANDER MONROE MCLEOD paced the small balcony outside his grandmother's room at the, to him, ridiculously named Palace of Peace and Contentment. The view from the balcony was breathtaking—the brilliant, shining blue-green sea of the Gulf of Thailand, small dark-sailed fishing vessels slowly going about their work, the bright sails of windsurfers from the resort across on the mainland flitting back and forth, and to the right infinite shades of green as thick rainforest ran riot over the sides of the mountain on which the palace was built.

In spite of the colourful and effusive brochures he'd read about the place, the marbled floors and silk-lined walls, he was reasonably sure it had never been a palace, let alone the summer home of long-dead kings of Siam. But it *had* been a very luxurious hotel, built when the village had been nothing more than a few shacks and some fishing boats. Built with its own generator for power and a permanent water supply from the spring further up the mountains.

The palace also explained his presence here. Bored out of his skull, but needing to stay—

His attention was momentarily diverted from his irritation with his situation by a woman. She was tall, long-limbed and straight-backed, with a mop of dark hair unhindered by a hat— foolish creature—and she was striding down the paved drive that ran through the perfectly kept gardens fragrant with frangipani and man- icured lawns he'd swear were clipped each morning with scissors—

To an assignation she had to keep, a desti- nation she wished to reach, or was she simply escaping the place?

Not that he could blame her.

But what lingered in his mind as she dis- appeared from view, where the drive curved slightly, was his first thought on seeing her— the totally absurd thought that she'd look good on a horse.

Look good on a horse?

He kicked the potted palm in one corner of the balcony and swore quietly to himself. Prolonged inactivity was obviously driving him insane. Or at least turning his brain to mush. He *had* to find something to do—something he could do without moving too far from the luxurious suite of rooms where his grandmother was dying—the same suite of rooms in which she had honeymooned with his late grandfather.

Returning here to die had been her one wish—her last wish, she'd said, probably to get him here—and although the extensive research he'd done on the place had shown him it was now actually a luxury convalescent home, he'd been doubtful. While a panel of specialists on the mainland advised on medical matters, top-class residential housekeeping, therapeutic and nursing staff made sure the guests—definitely not patients—were well cared for. His grandmother had three cheerful and gentle Thai nurses who attended to her personal needs—bathing, dressing, feeding her—with reverence and concern.

Pampered, more like! he thought with a derisive snort. The place was a luxurious convalescent facility for anyone wealthy enough to afford its exorbitant daily tariff.

Not that the money had been a problem when his grandmother had dropped her bombshell and demanded to die in the place where she had been so happy on her honeymoon. Her side of the family had always been wealthy, but a little app he'd fiddled around with during his student years had eventually been developed and sold. DocSays had brought him wealth beyond imagining in spite of the fact that the most important of the answers it gave anyone using it was, if in doubt, to see a doctor.

Could he update it?

Think of something new?

Or had that questing part of his brain atrophied as he'd practised the medicine for which he'd been training at the time?

But it was worth a try—anything to ease the boredom of waiting around.

If there'd been something he could do for his grandmother on a daily basis—if she'd been well enough to be wheeled out into the beautiful gardens, even taken for a ride in a little tuk-tuk—he'd have been more content.

It was the helplessness he felt—the fact that he, a doctor, could do nothing more to help the woman he loved so dearly—that was getting to him.

And that thought was also annoying—the one about loving her so dearly. She'd brought him up from the age of twelve, and her answer to any upset in his young life had always been, 'Monroes don't do emotion!'

Yet, if he gave himself time to think—and at the moment he had plenty—he had to accept that what he had always felt for her was love and that perhaps the stricture should have been, 'Monroes don't *show* emotion.'

His argument against it had been that he was a McLeod but she'd blown 'such nonsense' away with an airy wave.

'For all your name, you're a Monroe through and through, and don't you ever forget it,' she'd told him in a steely voice.

But seeing her now, turned from a strong, determined woman into frail bones and fine, lined, pale skin, he realised the pain he felt when he looked at her *had* to be emotion.

Love.

A love so deep it was as if part of himself was dying.

And repeating her words to himself—Monroes don't do emotion—did little to stop the pain…

He returned to his pacing, and caught the movement out of the corner of his eye. It was the woman who'd look good on horseback returning.

On a horse?

Hilary McKenzie Steele wasn't entirely sure she should be riding up the raked gravel drive of the Palace of Peace and Contentment, but Muriel Walker, her assigned 'guest', had told her about the stables.

'Beautiful horses, Kenzie dear,' she'd said. 'There for all of us to ride, but how many do? Do the horses get the exercise they need, do you think?'

'I'm sure they do,' Kenzie replied, aware of her position as a sounding board.

Not that Muriel was sick or in need of special nursing care, she was simply bored, moving from one luxurious home or hotel to another.

This luxury convalescent hotel had been on her itinerary for a few years, though why she always insisted on a nurse as a companion, Kenzie had yet to fathom.

Anything different to give her life a little meaning, Kenzie supposed.

Which explained the horse.

Muriel, for all her die-away airs and imaginary illnesses, was only in her early sixties, and, Kenzie was sure, could learn to ride a horse. Surely that would give her something to do.

Kenzie rode to the side entrance. She'd left Muriel in the little sitting room just off the side lobby—Muriel dressed in jeans and a light polo top, a deceptively simple outfit that had possibly cost as much as the horse.

Tethering Bob—Kenzie smiled again at the unlikely name for a Thai horse—she went inside to fetch Muriel.

'Come on,' she told the older woman. 'It's time you learned to ride.'

Muriel, who'd been resistant to the idea from the beginning, looked at Kenzie and must have read something in her face that told her argument would be futile.

She stood and then smiled.

'If I fall off I'll sack you,' she warned, and Kenzie, although not entirely sure her boss turned friend was joking, laughed.

Kenzie had given a lot of thought to getting Muriel onto the horse, and had come up with this side entrance as the ideal place. Not only would no one see them—she wasn't going to have anyone laughing at Muriel—but the urns that flanked the shallow steps were on a stepped platform. It had been simple enough to remove one of the urns, giving Muriel steps to get up and a flat area to stand on as she swung herself into the saddle.

Or perhaps clambered into the saddle…

She was helping Muriel with the transfer from the platform to the horse when a man appeared, turning the corner from the drive and stopping to watch the operation.

'Need a hand?'

Rich, deep, English tones made the three simple words ring through the air, hitting Kenzie's ears and somehow reverberating through her body in a way that brought heat to her cheeks.

Embarrassment at being caught?

She hoped that's all it was.

And cursed the colour that rose so easily. Honestly, you'd think by now she'd have outgrown blushing…

'We'll manage,' she said, but far too late, because now he was at the horse, steadying Muriel from the other side, putting her foot into the stirrup Kenzie had shortened earlier.

'First time?' he said, smiling up at Muriel.

The smile caused Kenzie more problems than the voice. She shook her head, trying to clear the sudden confusion. *Muriel.* She had to concentrate on Muriel, not some stranger with a beautiful voice.

Strange *man* at that and she was here to get over men...

For ever, if she had her way—but that was another problem altogether...

'Now you take the reins, and hold them so you just feel the horse's mouth at the end of them,' she told her charge.

'Just the left hand,' the stranger said, releasing Muriel's right hand from the folded reins. 'That's so you can carry the whip in your right and smack him if he's naughty.'

'Oh, I couldn't hit him,' Muriel protested, and the man laughed.

'Who are you?'

Kenzie was aware that the question came out far more forcibly—rudely?—than she'd intended, but the laughter had brought back her confusion.

He made a sweeping bow—to Muriel, not to her—and said, 'Alexander Monroe McLeod, prisoner in this palace, and happy to be of assistance.'

Another worker, Kenzie decided, although she certainly hadn't set eyes on him in the ten days she'd been here.

'Your grandmother?' Muriel asked him softly, and he nodded, and although some things fell into place—the talk of a woman who'd come here to die, her doctor grandson with her—something else was niggling at Kenzie.

She studied the man across the horse and frowned. She knew the face, and the name had rung a bell—several bells—but what…?

And shouldn't she introduce herself?

Some instinct pushed that thought away, though why, she couldn't tell.

'So,' he said, still speaking to Muriel. 'Where are we off to on this adventure?'

'Not very far,' Muriel assured him. 'In fact, I think getting on is enough for one day.'

'Nonsense,' the man—Alexander Monroe McLeod, how grand—said. 'You need to get the feel of the animal. So, if your friend leads and I stay right beside you on this side, will you feel safe enough?'

Muriel nodded tentatively and Kenzie flicked the lead rein very gently and clicked a 'Get up,' at the horse, who moved obediently and sedately along the path.

The man with the beautiful voice and grand name was talking quietly to Muriel, distracting her from the first-time rider's usual thoughts of how precarious her perch was and how very far away the ground!

Which gave Kenzie the time to sneak glances at him across the horse's neck.

She was sure she knew the name but definitely hadn't met him. Tall, dark-haired, distinguished-looking somehow, with the kind of profile you could put on a coin.

It was such a fanciful thought she had to give herself a stern reminder that she was here to forget a man, not to be fancying a new one, no matter how attractive he was.

Yet he wasn't the kind of man you'd forget!

Perhaps she'd seen a photograph?

Lightbulb moment!

'I know who you are,' she said, unable to

keep a note of triumph from her voice. 'You're the bloke who developed the DocSays app!'

'What did you say?' Muriel was obviously mystified.

'Do you know it?' he asked, the question a trifle stiff.

Kenzie laughed.

'I doubt there's a nurse in the world who doesn't. Working in a hospital can be a bit humdrum at times, so we often see what you'd say about our patients' symptoms. Harmless fun, and as you always say see a doctor, that's actually what's happening with our patients, if you see what I mean.'

Alex stared at the woman in total disbelief.

'You compare your actual hospital doctor's diagnosis with the app?'

'It's fun!' she had the hide to say, before adding, 'They're usually the same.'

As if *that* made a difference! Nurses comparing his opinions to those of other doctors as if it was a game…

'Who are *you*?' he demanded, thrown off balance by this whole situation—the horse, his earlier, and definitely weird, thoughts about the woman, and a laughing face with blue eyes that were rather startling against her lightly tanned skin.

'I'm Hilary McKenzie Steele,' she announced, undoubtedly mimicking his own introduction. 'Known to one and all as Kenzie! My mother died in childbirth and Dad gave me her whole name, so that's my excuse for its length.'

She was making fun of him, he knew, but he *had* introduced himself with his full name when Alex McLeod would have done. And all he could offer by way of explanation for its length were hundreds of years of tradition—rather feeble compared to a dead mother.

'Are you still ready to catch me if I fall?' Muriel asked, breaking into his senseless thoughts.

'I most certainly am,' he said. 'But tell me how you feel. Comfortable—'

'Or terrified?' the woman called Kenzie asked, with a smile in her voice that made it a gentle tease.

'Well, it *is* a long way up, but it feels just fine,' Muriel assured them. 'Can we go on down the drive—maybe right to the stables?'

'Of course,' Kenzie replied, although Alex felt a slight unease about this decision. He hadn't even known—or if he had he'd forgotten—there were stables and horses, but how far away were they?

'Um, Kenzie,' he said, tentatively trying the name on his lips and finding he quite liked it. 'I'm not sure I can stay much longer.'

'Oh, that's okay,' she answered cheerfully. 'You can see Muriel has her balance now and there's a dismounting block at the stables. Do you ride yourself? There are some lovely horses in the stables, and apparently there are trails up through the rainforest towards the top of the mountain.'

'And you've been here how long?' he demanded, aggrieved that the blue-eyed woman apparently knew so much about the place.

'Ten days! But I guess us menials mix with locals more than you guests do. This place is very upstairs downstairs, isn't it?'

'Oh, Kenzie,' Muriel murmured. 'I don't make you feel like that, do I?'

Kenzie laughed.

'Of course not, you silly goose. I was just teasing.'

'Teasing *me*,' Alex muttered, before looking up at Muriel.

'Are you sure you feel safe with just Kenzie here beside you?'

Muriel smiled down at him.

'Of course,' she said. 'Hasn't Kenzie already proven her worth, showing me how nice it is to be on a horse? Maybe one day, when I can ride by myself—Kenzie's going to teach me—we can all ride up into the mountains.'

She paused, still looking at him.

'That's if you can ride, of course.'

He wanted to snort. He'd practically been born on a horse! But he confined himself to a polite goodbye to both women, and hurried back into the hotel. Even when his grandmother was awake, she was barely conscious and a lot of that time had no idea who he was.

Which, of course, made him very reluctant to miss any moments with her when she did! He thought of the times he *hadn't* spent with her. Breaking a lunch or dinner arrangement because he was held up at the hospital, or, worse, out on a date, such ordinary things, but all time he had already missed with her.

And now there was no time to make it up to her—no more time…

But as he went up in the lift, he couldn't help

picturing his first glimpse of the woman with the improbable name—long legs striding easily, back straight, and the cloud of dark hair—black, he thought now, or perhaps a very dark brown.

And the explanation for these thoughts?

He had absolutely no idea and the sooner he got them out of his head the better. Since the farcical end of his engagement and marriage plans he'd remained aloof to the charms of women, throwing himself into work as an alternative—and far easier—passion.

He shook his head in a futile attempt to remove the wayward meanderings of his mind. It was because he was stressed. He couldn't do anything for Gran, and doing nothing left him with too much time on his hands to dwell on life without her...

But, then, she *had* looked good on the horse... Kenzie...

The rest of Muriel's ride was uneventful, but Kenzie was glad to see a little tuk-tuk waiting to take her and her charge back to the hotel.

'You should have a hot shower, and I'll arrange a massage for you,' she said to Muriel as they climbed into the little rickshaw. 'You might need another one tomorrow, too, because your muscles have been doing something new.'

'Then I'll have to have a massage every day,' Muriel announced, 'because I'm going to conquer this horse-riding thing!'

'You're a Trojan, Muriel!' Kenzie told her, 'But you might be sore tomorrow so we'll take it easy.'

She saw Muriel safely back to her room and into the shower, arranged the massage, and ordered tea and scones for after it.

Only then did she pull out her phone and open the DocSays app on it. She had to smile at the pixelated image of Alexander Monroe McLeod, which looked, of course, nothing like him. The photos she'd seen occasionally—usually on the financial pages of serious papers—was how she'd recognised him.

Imagine meeting the man!

Her friends would never believe it!

Especially the ones who'd told her she was crazy to take a short contract job at a luxury convalescent home off the coast of Thailand.

'You'll be bored to death,' they'd warned her, and secretly she'd believed them, but at the time she'd have taken a job on Mars to get away from her far too small home town!

Small town, new doctor, whirlwind romance that had the entire town speculating whether Kenzie would finally get married, then the new doc's wife had arrived…

Kenzie had expected pain—and hurt pride and humiliation had certainly brought that in its train. But in many ways it had been a relief. Much as she wanted to marry and have children—and urgent as that need was becoming—she'd known all along there was something not quite right about Mark…

Something that had, thankfully, held her back from a physical relationship with him…

'Now, Kenzie,' Muriel announced, appearing from the bathroom in a cloud of steam and a luxurious peignoir, 'I will have no argument about it this time. You are to eat with me this evening. We need to plan out my riding lessons.'

'It might be best to leave any plans until morning. See how you feel then.'

'We can discuss it over dinner,' Muriel said forcefully.

So much for diversion!

'I thought the Sapphire Dining Room tonight. It's smaller and for all they tell me the same chef oversees both kitchens, I'm sure the food is better there.'

They *had* argued before about Kenzie dining with her guest, as a cleverly worded sentence in the rules and regulations for ancillary staff seemed to suggest it wasn't a good idea.

And certainly not on any regular basis!

Feeling obliged to protest, Kenzie offered her usual excuse.

'But it's formal, Muriel, you know that, and you also know that I packed for a job on a tropical island, not a luxury escape.'

A light tap on the door interrupted the argument.

'That'll be the masseuse. Let her in, and put out my medication, then go and find something to wear. Shall we say my room, at seven? We can have a drink before we go down.'

As the masseuse was already setting up her table, Kenzie dealt out the evening tablets—blood-pressure medication, statins for her high cholesterol, and tonight a weekly tablet to maintain her bone density. She put them all into a small medicine cup, set a glass of water beside it, and left the room.

Idly, as the elevator descended to the ground floor, she wondered if DocSays ate in one of the dining rooms—specifically, the Sapphire?

She pushed the thought away—she was off men—and concentrated on clothes.

If she could find a tuk-tuk outside the palace, she'd have time to get down to the markets in the little village. Not that formal wear was a common feature on any of the stalls, but if she could find a pretty sarong that went with one of her tank tops, she could tie it around her waist and look at least presentable.

The sarong was a light, gauzy cotton in swirling shades of blue, green and purple. With a silky, black tank top and her good black sandals, it would do at a push, but the idea of eating in a formal dining room with the wealthy guests of the palace was daunting to a girl from the bush, where formal meant wearing something on your feet.

Muriel was delighted to see her, admiring her outfit and her nous in achieving it. She poured a small glass of champagne for each of them and toasted the success of her first riding 'lesson'.

They went down to dinner arm in arm, Muriel sweeping Kenzie into the dining room as if she were a close friend.

And Kenzie found herself pleased to have Muriel with her, for the grandeur of the place—the s*maller* dining room at that—was almost overwhelming. She'd grown used to the beautiful grand entrance with its gold-streaked black marble floors, the potted orchids peeping from behind soft ferns, but this was something else.

It lived up to its name of sapphire, for it was decorated, almost entirely, in blue. Pale eggshell-blue walls that looked as if they were lined with velvet, darker blue upholstered chairs that made the white napery look so much more vivid. And the crystal glassware on the table sparkled, refracting light from the elegant chandelier into thousands of bright, winking, stars.

Hadn't Muriel read the line about ancillary staff knowing their place? This was definitely not Kenzie's place...

But of course Muriel wouldn't have read it! As if she would read something as insignificant as a brochure.

But the maître d' was probably word perfect in it. He raised one perfectly trimmed eyebrow, and would have led them to a table in the far corner had Muriel not protested and insisted she sit by the window.

'Oh, and there's that nice man!' she cried in delight. 'Let's ask him to join us.'

The eyebrow rose again, and Kenzie managed to mumble, 'Dr McLeod,' to prevent further strain to the small arc of hair.

And for all she'd hoped the invitation would be refused, as she slipped into her seat she saw him rise and cross the room towards them.

He smiled down at Muriel and raised the glass of red wine he held in one hand in a silent toast.

'So, how was the rest of your ride?' he asked.

'Wonderful! Great fun! I'm doing it again and next time Kenzie will ride beside me and still hold the leading rein, but that's just for safety.'

Kenzie opened her mouth to protest that they might be taking things a little too fast, but Muriel's raised hand stopped any protest.

'I haven't got time to be footling around in a

paddock for days on end,' she said. 'I want to be a rider, which means I need to hurry things along.'

Alex took the chair a waiter had pulled to the table for him, and smiled at the two women. He had a feeling the younger of them wished he'd declined the invitation, yet it was she he'd been drawn towards—wanting to see her again, speak to her.

Was it a symptom of his boredom that the young woman intrigued him so much? Laughing at the nurses' use of his app, introducing herself in an echo of his stuffy announcement of his own name?

Or was it that she was just so attractive?

Naturally attractive, just herself, with no apparent effort to attract—

Well, maybe a little lipstick on beautifully shaped lips, a touch of eyeliner accentuating the smiling blue eyes, but none of the studied and worked-at perfection of most of the women he knew.

Whatever it was, she'd somehow awoken something inside him—something he'd always doubted existed...

There was certainly something about her...

But Muriel was his hostess.

'I'm called Alex,' he said to her. 'I don't think I ever did that proper introduction, and I know you're Muriel. Are you here convalescing?'

She smiled her sunny smile.

'You could say that. I did have a small operation—just the smallest of tucks, you know—but really it's a break from my usual life, which, until I got up close and personal with a horse today, had become very boring, and sometimes seemed totally pointless.'

'And the horse has changed all that?' Alex teased gently, and the woman virtually glowed with delight.

'But of course it has!' she said. 'Kenzie tells me there are horses I can hire to ride in Central Park in New York, and even Hyde Park in London. I can ride just about anywhere!'

'Have you ridden in these places?' Alex asked, turning to bring the woman for whom he'd changed tables into the conversation.

She smiled at him, curving pink lips to reveal perfect teeth, a smile dancing in the blue eyes.

'Not yet,' she said, 'but it's definitely waiting for me in the future.'

'Bucket list?'

'I don't think people my age are too worried about bucket lists,' she said, a little frown turning the words serious. 'I'm more into planning my immediate future right now.'

'Which is?'

He wasn't sure why he'd asked.

Politeness?

Not that she gave him time to ponder such things, coming out with, 'Getting married and having children,' with such alacrity he was taken aback.

'It's not *my* ambition,' Kenzie continued, trying to explain the unexpected response she'd given to his question, partly because it had shocked her as much as her dinner companions.

'My *ambition* was to become a surgical nurse, not that that could ever happen when I also wanted to work as close as possible to my home, and small country hospitals don't have surgeons.'

She paused before adding, 'Well, we do have the flying surgeon come in every six weeks, but he brings his own nurse. Anyway, now my family situation has changed I've got to do something about producing a couple of children, and my father would prefer it if they were legitimate, hence the marriage part.'

She shrugged, as if her explanation needed no further trimmings.

'I quite understand your father's feelings,' Muriel said, breaking the silence this far too personal statement had produced, but as Alex could find no follow-up it wasn't broken for long.

A waiter saved the day, arriving to collect the menus and take orders, but as the menus were still unopened on the table, Muriel waved him away.

She also took charge, telling them both to decide what they were eating so they could get back to Kenzie's problem.

'It's hardly a problem,' Kenzie retorted, then blushed and looked down at her menu, adding, in a very small voice, 'Well, I suppose it is in a way.'

She looked positively woebegone, but before he could assure her she'd have no trouble finding any number of men to marry, Muriel interrupted with a stern, 'Decide what you want to eat!'

Having been raised by his grandmother, obedience to older women was second nature to Alex, so he perused the menu and decided on a *meen molee*—fish curry, delicately simmered in coconut milk, according to the menu.

'I'm not that adventurous,' Kenzie said, 'but the green chicken curry sounds delicious.'

Muriel opted for the yellow vegetarian curry and when the waiter appeared asked him for enough rice for all three of them.

'And wine, of course—no, make it champagne. Kenzie and I had a little toast earlier, but we need a full bottle with you here, Alex.'

Alex smiled to himself. It could have been his grandmother talking, never thinking to ask his preference—never imagining, he sometimes thought—that it could possibly differ from hers, bless her.

But he felt a twinge of sadness at the thought. His mother had died far too young, leaving him to be brought up by his grandmother. She'd been strict about his keeping to the values of his name—the Monroe name, of course—but always fair, and ready to support him whatever path he took in life.

She hadn't been a physically demonstrative woman—not a hugger, and only rarely did he get a kiss, but he'd always known she loved him deeply, as, indeed, he'd loved her.

And now she was going too, and a large part of his life would go with her.

He shook away the sadness his thoughts produced. Monroes didn't do emotion!

'And are you here to further your father's ambition?'

He'd been lost in thoughts of his maternal relative, so wasn't sure if Muriel's question had been thrown at him.

Fortunately, Kenzie was quicker on the uptake.

'No!' she said firmly. 'This is just a short break to recharge and regroup. I'll get on to it when I get home.'

'You make it sound like a military operation,' he teased, hoping to see the smile again.

'Well, not exactly,' she said earnestly. 'But I've learned you do have to be careful. People are marrying later, and while an older man—say, in his thirties—would be fine, most of them have regular girlfriends by then.'

'Thirties is old?' Alex asked, thinking he'd always considered his own age—thirty-five—as still young, not yet middle-aged, let alone old.

'How old are you?' he asked, and now she did smile.

'Twenty-six, but that's not the point. I know it probably sounds ridiculous to you, but my mother died when I was born, and for years I've just kept hoping that my father would marry again and have more children. And now he's finally fallen in love again but with an older woman—so no children—which leaves it up to me to keep the family business going.'

She paused, studying him as if to make sure he was following.

'It's the property, you see,' she said. 'It's been in the family for six generations—through drought and fires and floods—and was built with the blood and sweat and tears of my ancestors. It's in our lifeblood, and my father desperately wants it to keep going. We have a resident manager, and I'll run it with him if something happens to my father, but it's the next generation. I really need to produce them while my father can pass on all his knowledge and the history of the place.'

'Which a manager couldn't do,' Muriel put in. 'They'd never feel for things the way the family would."

Kenzie nodded.

'Or care for it the way the family would,' she said. 'We run fifteen thousand head of cattle—Brahmans—up the gulf. They're a lot of work—we breed them ourselves, castrate them when they're young, then shift them around according to where the feed is. And then there's the breeding stock—we turn off about eight thousand a year so you need to re-place them—and then there are decisions for the future—drought-proofing, seeking out new markets when prices slump.'

As she'd rattled off all this information, Alex had tried desperately to keep up. The 'prop-erty' he'd envisaged had been a large house, or maybe a business of some sort—but fifteen thousand cattle plus enough breeders to 'turn off'—presumably to sell—eight thousand a year?

'I see!' he said, rather vaguely as he had no idea how to relate to all this information.

Fortunately, Muriel took up the conversa-tional ball.

'My second husband had Brahmans—ugly big things they were, too. That dreadful hump. He bred them, took them to shows, won ribbons, which was nice because when he died they put the ribbons on his coffin instead of flowers, which just die anyway.'

By the time Alex had digested this bit of conversation, he was wondering why on earth he'd agreed to join the table. He'd been eating on his own quite happily for two weeks.

He could excuse himself, say he had to check on his grandmother and he'd have his meal sent up, but he knew it would be a lie as her coma-like sleep had deepened late this afternoon and he knew she wouldn't wake before morning.

Beside which, meeting this slim, upright young woman with the sparkling smile and laughing blue eyes, who'd apparently grown up with fifteen thousand cattle, had certainly banished his boredom. The frank way she spoke of her home and her need to have children to carry on a family tradition not only intrigued him, but it touched on something deep inside him.

The concept of family, he supposed—a concept his grandmother considered of the utmost importance.

So instead of reading stories by solemn Scottish writers to Gran in the morning, he could entertain her with stories of cattle farms.

Cattle properties?

CHAPTER TWO

KENZIE WASN'T SURE exactly when it was that she'd realised she was enjoying herself, but the first courses had arrived and as they ate, Muriel regaled them with tales of her husbands, Alex demanded more information on cattle with humps, and she'd forgotten the humiliation that had sent her scurrying over here.

But the fling had taught her an important lesson. When she returned to her quest, it wasn't enough to take up with a good-looking man who could charm the socks—and probably other bits of apparel—off a woman, she had to be sure he had a serious side, and hadn't crossed marriage off his to-do list.

Or been already married…

For her, getting married had to be a business decision! Nothing more, nothing less!

Too much attraction just got in the way of seeing a person for who he was—or wasn't, as it had happened…

And who's to say they wouldn't grow to love each other? Friendship grew from small beginnings, so couldn't love?

'Oh, this is the famous soprano who's staying here.'

Muriel's comment roused Kenzie from her thoughts, and she turned to see a rather magnificent woman take the small stage.

'She's here for a rest, and was going to sing earlier in the week but had a cold. I've heard her sing in Milan—she's really superb.'

Glad to be diverted from thoughts of seriously suitable men, Kenzie sat back in her chair and lifted her glass to sip her champagne.

The pianist provided an introduction and then the woman's beautiful voice soared around the room, filling it with both sound and emotion.

Kenzie checked that both her companions were absorbed and took a moment to have another look at the genius behind DocSays.

Not considering him as a potential partner—tech billionaires were way out of her league—she could barely handle her internet banking!

Although he *was* attractive! Attractive to her

certainly—that strange spark she'd felt when they'd first met over the horse...

But hadn't she just decided she wasn't looking for attraction? Attraction could mask other more important things, like a man's being married, or not wanting to be married, and you ended up wasting time on the wrong man.

Besides which, he'd hardly want to move to a place in the middle of nowhere, with its endless sky and red soil plains and—

She cut off the thought before she got too nostalgic—better to think about the genius behind DocSays!

He was a good-looking man—a Scot, from his names, but very English-looking to her, maybe because he was wearing a suit to dinner on a tropical island...

But looking around the room, other men were similarly attired and they didn't look particularly English. More American, she decided, although the man in a dinner jacket might be Greek.

She'd returned her attention to their dinner companion—purely a research thing—so saw the moment he moved, standing up so suddenly he knocked his chair over, and strode to the front of the room.

Where the soprano had stopped singing and was now lying crumpled on the stage.

Training had Kenzie following, arriving by the fallen woman to hear Alex mutter, 'Not breathing—epiglottitis,' then yell, 'Call an ambulance, and someone get a sharp thin-tipped knife from the kitchen and some tubing—straws, anything.'

As a waiter dashed off to the kitchen, Kenzie looked quickly around, aware the woman's neck would need to be supported.

The pianist had a cushion on his chair!

She dashed across and practically snatched it from under him, leaving the shocked man staring at the drama.

'Thank you,' Alex muttered at her as she helped him roll the woman onto her back.

She slid the cushion under the singer's neck, stretching it so Alex could more easily feel for the position for the first vertical cut he would need to make beneath the Adam's apple, and the second transverse cut through the cricothyroid membrane.

His fingers moved with such certainty she knew he was good and the woman had been extremely lucky he'd been in the audience.

The waiter returned with a razor-sharp knife in one hand and a piece of plastic tubing dangling in the other. Kenzie wondered just what it might be used for in the kitchen.

As Alex took the knife, he gestured for Kenzie to take the tube.

'About five centimetres,' he told her, and she grabbed the tube and a clean knife off a table and cut off a long enough piece for Alex to insert into the wound he was making.

She held it as she squatted on the other side of the singer, ready to hand it to him when the cuts were made.

'Just hold her steady,' he said to Kenzie, and she moved to the woman's head and held it gently but firmly while Alex inserted the tube. He blew briefly into it, watching to make sure the chest rose and fell.

Tension thickened the air.

The tube was in place, but would the woman breathe?

Alex had moved his hands ready to do chest

compressions when a slight whistling sound told them she was breathing on her own.

'Well done,' Kenzie said to him. 'But what happened?'

Alex's eyes didn't move from his patient.

'According to Muriel, she's had a cold. Possibly a throat infection, and her epiglottis was swollen enough to close right up when she sang. Silly thing to do—she should have continued to rest.'

Kenzie nodded.

'But you still picked up on it very quickly. Do you still do hands-on medicine?'

He smiled at the surprise in her voice. It wasn't the first time he'd heard it.

'Of course I do! I can hardly just sit around counting the money my app made. I worked hard for a long time to finish my degree and I certainly wouldn't let it go to waste. I work in an A and E department. To tell you the truth, I'm probably addicted to emergency medicine. For me, it's the ultimate job—the pace of it— the rush!'

'Tell me about it,' Kenzie muttered. 'My rotations through the ED when I was training were the stuff of nightmares.'

'Ah, but your pet hate is probably not boredom. For me there's nothing worse.'

An ambulance arrived, and although the paramedics accompanying the stretcher had efficiently replaced the kitchen tubing with a tracheostomy tube, inflated the cuff and secured it before moving the patient onto the stretcher, he was caught in a dilemma.

Should he go with her to the hospital? Make sure someone there knew what they were doing?

He glanced at his watch and must have been frowning for the young woman, Kenzie, touched him lightly on the shoulder.

'I'll go to the hospital and make sure she's in good hands,' she said. 'If you could explain to Muriel, she'll understand. I'm actually supposed to be off duty, but somehow we don't seem to do hours or set timetables, just hang out together. Tell her if I'm late getting back I'll see her in the morning. She's perfectly healthy but pays for a nurse—I think to keep her company.'

The blue eyes lifted to his.

'How terrible is that?'

The words were little more than a sigh, but Alex understood what she meant. Muriel, for all her money—and there must be plenty for her to be staying here—was lonely.

As are you, an inner voice whispered deep inside him. He didn't bother denying it—he'd had plenty of time to think these last couple of weeks—and for all he had friends and colleagues back in the ED where he worked, he had slowly come to realise that he'd made his work his life.

Relationships had broken down because of it.

Or because they hadn't been strong enough in the first place?

Because Monroes didn't do emotion?

Or, as one departing woman had told him, he was obsessed, but unfortunately not with her.

It was the boredom thing again! He'd tried other medical fields, thinking at first that surgery would give him the rush he needed, but it had lacked that immediacy—that often-fine line between life and death.

And a psychologist would probably tell him it was because he'd virtually witnessed that line as a child—waving goodbye to his parents who had been, within minutes, dead...

Pushing these memories aside, he slipped into the organised chaos of the kitchen to safely dispose of the knife and wash his hands, then stopped at Muriel's table.

'Kenzie's going to the hospital, but I'll be back to eat with you as soon as I've checked on my grandmother.'

Muriel shook her head.

'I really don't need someone dancing attendance on me all day, every day,' she said. 'I just enjoy the company of young people and with no children or grandchildren I'm quite happy to pay for the pleasure of their company.'

She paused, then added, 'And if I ask for a nurse I know she'll at least be university educated, so intelligent and easy to talk to, because that's part of being a nurse, wouldn't you say?'

Never having considered it before, Alex thought for a moment, then nodded. It was certainly true of hospital nurses who had to do the greater part of the communication with the patients. Doctors might come by, but were usually too rushed to explain things in any depth.

And in the ED it was the nurses who kept

everything running, if not always smoothly, at least with some attempt at order.

His grandmother remained stubbornly asleep, but he sat beside her anyway, as he did at this time every evening, and read a few pages of the latest book to her. At the moment, it was Robert Louis Stevenson's *Kidnapped*, and as he spoke the words his mind went back to when she'd read to him. All the books she'd read had been by her beloved Scottish authors, although he'd by far have preferred a scary story!

After a brief stay with no response, he returned to eat his meal with Muriel. He'd read again later, if only to stop himself thinking of the woman with the laughing blue eyes.

And fifteen thousand head of cattle.

He could understand that it would have taken…was it five generations of her family to build up such a massive property holding? His own McLeod family—closely related to the clan chief at Skye—went back about twenty generations but, apart from a few enterprising adventurers, most of them had idled away their fortunes rather than amassing wealth.

But he *was* titular head of his other Scottish clan—of the Monroes, not the McLeods—and

Kenzie's words about marriage and children had prodded his conscience. His responsibility as an only child was to continue the line, a fact that had been drummed into his head at an early age.

'It's up to you!' and 'Only you can do it!' were frequent refrains early on from his mother, and later his grandmother—the women in his family being familiar with the power of subtle blackmail.

And then, on his twelfth birthday, he'd actually promised. He'd been given his first grown-up kilt and a sporran with the Monroe crest on it.

The fact that he was actually a McLeod carried no weight with either of them, and in his best, grown-up voice, he'd promised.

He thought of the woman with the laughing blue eyes—the woman looking for a husband and two children.

Kill two birds with one stone?

Marriages of convenience were hardly uncommon in the history of his family, keen to keep as much inherited wealth as possible—even better if they could add to it.

He shook his head, smiling to himself, imagining Kenzie at a McLeod clan dinner in Dunvegan Castle, chatting on about breeding stock and castrating the young steers. He could almost feel the wince that would go around the family gathered at the chief's table!

No, there were plenty of suitable, marriageable women back home, even if the one he'd planned to marry had married someone else when he'd brought his grandmother out here. And kept the engagement ring, *and* worn the wedding dress intended for their wedding when she'd wed a friend of his.

'Well, it would only have gone to waste, wouldn't it, darling?'

He winced himself at the remembered conversation, possibly because, for all the talk of how suitable the match had been, he'd been silly enough to believe she'd loved him.

Even fancied himself in love with her for a while, although somehow he'd always known there was something missing between them.

Guessed it was to do with him and the difficulty he had in showing emotion.

'Are you married?'

Muriel's conversational opening threw him

for a moment. Had the woman been reading his thoughts?

'No, no ring, see!' he said, holding up both hands.

'Not all men wear rings,' Muriel told him. 'While some take them off when it's convenient.'

'Well, I don't have a white mark,' Alex pointed out, holding his left hand across the table for her inspection.

'Something wrong with your hand?'

Kenzie had returned, slipping into her seat as she spoke.

'The staff at the hospital weren't exactly hostile, but I think they thought I was trying to tell them their jobs so I made a quick exit. It's a small place but seems very efficient and apparently has a helicopter available on the roof if a patient needs to be transferred to the mainland.'

The explanation had been offered to both of them, but Muriel ignored it.

'I was checking he wasn't married,' she told Kenzie—about as subtle as a brick. 'He's not!'

'Well, good for him!' Kenzie said, although Alex saw the quick colour rise in her cheeks and guessed only ingrained politeness had held her temper in check.

Fortunately, their main course arrived, Muriel explaining she'd asked the kitchen to hold the dishes back.

'Because you do both have to eat, don't you?'

They ate, conversation limited for a while to comments on their meals, until Muriel managed to twist the talk back to Alex's single status.

'Well, what do you think?' Muriel demanded of Kenzie. 'Here he is, a single man, just what you're looking for.'

'Really, Muriel, you're embarrassing both of us,' Kenzie protested although she knew the colour in her cheeks would already have revealed her embarrassment—*and* the wretched man was smirking! 'I don't intend to throw myself at every single man that comes along— that's not how things work.'

'Well, it's worked for me,' Muriel said, with a mischievous smile, 'but if you've got some other plan, I'm sure we'd both like to hear it.'

Kenzie felt the heat burning now in her cheeks.

She did have a kind of plan and it would probably be helpful to talk about it, but—

'Come on, I know you want to talk about it!'

She pressed her palms to her scarlet cheeks and plunged right in.

'Okay, you'll both probably laugh at this but I thought I'd try internet dating,' she said. 'Everyone seems to be doing it these days. You get matched up with people who might be suitable and you get the chance to talk to them on the net for a while, then if you think you'd like to meet up, you start with meeting for a coffee and take it from there.'

Her voice trailed off as she finished because she had no idea about the 'take it from there' part.

'Do you hope for a spark of some kind to take it from there?' Alex asked, and Kenzie had to smile.

'I always get stuck at that part! Actually, I usually get stuck at the meeting for coffee part because it's unlikely I'll be matched up with anyone from my own town, so I'd have to arrange to meet in a regional centre, and once I've driven a couple of hundred kilometres to the coffee shop, I'm likely to be very narky if he's a dud.'

'If you have to travel that far, you could arrange to have a few that you could meet on the same day so it wasn't all wasted,' Alex suggested, definitely hiding a smirk!

'Oh, right! So, I'd flit from one coffee shop to the next—it all feels a bit like trying on clothes, doesn't it?'

'Nonsense!' Muriel declared. 'I've heard it's a very common and successful way for people to meet these days.'

Which could have ended the conversation had not Alex joined in.

'You could get started while you're here. Get your name into the system, so you can start being matched up. You can even do the internet chatting part from here and leave the actual meetings until you get home,' he said, every helpful suggestion a tease to see her squirm.

He was alleviating his boredom at her expense—that's what it was!

'I was only thinking about it,' Kenzie muttered as the subject veered out of her control.

'Nonsense!'

This was Muriel now, obviously caught up in the idea.

'We'll get on with it tomorrow after my riding lesson. Write your profile—isn't that what they ask for? Oh, this will be such fun!'

'Won't it just!' Alex put in.

'And you can help,' Muriel said to him. 'It will be very good to have a male perspective on it, won't it, Kenzie?'

As the ground beneath her failed to open up and swallow her whole to hide her embarrassment, Kenzie fought back.

'Alex won't want to be away from his grandmother for that long,' she said firmly, looking him in the eyes and daring him to argue.

Some dare!

The wretched man actually smiled—no doubt at her still scarlet cheeks—and said, oh, so casually, 'Oh, I'm sure something could be arranged. I'm often on the computer while I sit with her, and I have a pager so I can always be called back.'

He then added a devastating smile that reduced Kenzie to a boneless lump of ectoplasm, and left the room.

Ridiculous! It was embarrassment causing the consternation inside her—nothing more.

Kenzie glared at the door through which he'd vanished, then stood up.

'Come along, Muriel, it's time we left, too.'

She moved to Muriel's side, taking the older woman's elbow to steady her as they walked towards the door, although she knew that Muriel didn't need support.

Kenzie lay in the comfortable bed in the smaller bedroom of Muriel's suite. At times like this she'd have been happier staying in the staff quarters where she took her meals if Muriel didn't require her. At least there she'd have had company—other young people to talk to, a bit of light-hearted chat, nothing more.

But no! It hadn't taken her long to realise that the hotel had hired her as a companion for Muriel, rather than a nurse, although many of the guests did bring their own nurses.

But a companion's role was very different. Hadn't Muriel emphasised that point with the evening's very personal conversation about her, Kenzie's, future?

Once *that* idea, which had still been in its infancy in Kenzie's head, was out in the open, Muriel had leapt on it like another new challenge. Horse riding was all well and good, but couldn't go on all day, so sorting out Kenzie's life would appeal to Muriel as a very pleasant diversion.

But dragging Alex into it?

That was just sheer embarrassment.

He probably wouldn't join them!

Why on earth would he?

She shifted to ease the swirly feeling in her stomach and settled into sleep.

Muriel's second lesson was a great success. Probably, as far as Kenzie was concerned, because Alex hadn't appeared!

The man made her nervous—or maybe unsettled was a better description of the sensations she'd been feeling in his presence.

Because he was attractive?

Or because she found him so?

She shut her mind against all thoughts of him. She was here to take a break from men…

They'd decided to hold the lesson in the enclosed paddock behind the stables, which was basically for children and beginner riders. After a couple of rounds of the paddock, Muriel insisted Kenzie relinquish the leading rein, and around she rode, ramrod straight, her face radiant with joy at her achievement.

'I'll ride back up to the hotel to show Alex,' she announced after these successful solo efforts, but Kenzie had visions of a car or a little noisy tuk-tuk coming up the drive and spooking the horse, for all the animal was very docile.

'Not on your second lesson,' Kenzie told her. 'Perhaps, if you feel like a ride this afternoon, he might find time to accompany you on one of the short trails.'

'With you, too, Kenzie,' Muriel insisted.

Kenzie smiled at her.

'I think you might find I'm due a bit of time off,' she said. 'Not that anyone working with you really needs time off as you're so generous about sharing your adventures. But I need to email my dad and do some washing—just little things.'

Best not to mention she'd given some thought to Muriel's suggestion—or had it been Alex's?—that she might as well begin her sortie into the world of internet dating while she was here. First she had to see what the different sites offered, and the kind of profiles people supplied.

What on earth could *she* put on a profile?

Nurse, handy with cattle—

They took a tuk-tuk back to the hotel, where Kenzie once again arranged a massage for Muriel, then left to have some 'you time', as Muriel called it.

'But be back at six for a chat and a drink,' Muriel insisted. 'I know you're uncomfortable about eating with me, but we can still have a drink before dinner.'

Kenzie restrained a groan. In spite of the previous day's champagne, Muriel's aperitif of choice was a very dry martini, sent up to the room already mixed in an elaborate silver shaker, olives on sticks in a little bowl.

As far as Kenzie was concerned, it was a very old-fashioned drink, but Muriel had her particular likes and dislikes and she stuck by them.

Hating the taste but unwilling to spoil Muriel's fun, Kenzie had become adept at sharing them with the nearest flower arrangement. She was surreptitiously disposing of half a glass when there was a tap on the door and in walked Alex.

'Be a dear and phone room service,' Muriel said to him. 'We want another shaker of these. I've already had them send up a glass for you.'

So Kenzie didn't like martinis, Alex thought as he obediently picked up the phone to order more. From the doorway, it had been easy to see her tipping some into the flowers, but where would she get rid of the next one if he sat between her and the flowers?

It had to be boredom that his mind had even suggested such a ploy, but that wouldn't make it less fun.

The new cocktails arrived, the room-service waiter filling all three glasses.

'You don't like olives?' he teased as Kenzie waved the plate away.

'Spoils the gin,' she said quickly, but he knew her mind was elsewhere, her eyes searching the room for a likely hiding spot for the refreshed drink.

'Have you had any ideas?'

Muriel's question took his mind off Kenzie, which was probably a very good thing as she was dressed in a soft blue shirt with two pockets that seemed to emphasise shapely breasts, and some of her night-dark hair—shining as if newly washed—hung almost to the pockets, while those blue eyes were shielded by her fringe—

'Well?'

Maybe Muriel's first question hadn't quite worked.

'Don't know much about it,' he said, fixing his attention on Muriel so he wouldn't be distracted again. 'But I did read up about it on the net and it seems you should write something a bit quirky and fun, and ask a question to encourage the reader to get back to you.'

'What kind of question?' Kenzie demanded, and he looked back to see her glass half-empty.

Had she actually drunk it?

He peered around—no handbag she could have tipped it into, not that she would, surely. Think of the mess!

And the carpet near her feet seemed dry enough.

But the feet were slim and shapely, *and* in sandals—

'The question,' the feet's owner prompted.

He looked up, met her eyes, wondered momentarily why his mouth felt dry, and smiled to cover the fact that he'd completely lost the conversational thread.

Muriel caught on first.

'What kind of questions should Kenzie ask?'

Valiantly pulling his head back on track, although the disappearance of the martini still intrigued him, he said, 'Well, say you put in that you like classical music, then you might ask what music they like.'

Kenzie smiled—a smile so sweetly innocent he knew he was in trouble.

'And if I say I like horses do I add, "What horses do you like?"'

'You know exactly what I mean!' Alex said crossly, unable to believe he was letting this woman he barely knew get under his skin.

Or, for that matter, that he was sitting here discussing what a woman—a total stranger—should put in her internet dating profile.

Internet dating—the whole idea was ridiculous. She could end up with anyone! Who knew what lies men would tell to get set up with a woman—especially a woman as attractive as

Kenzie? Presumably she'd have to put up a photo of herself...

He shook his head to clear it of his meandering—and disquieting—thoughts. He'd obviously been even more bored than he'd realised!

'Come on, you two, it will be time for dinner soon, and we've got nothing done.' Muriel handed Kenzie a pen and notepad. 'Now, start writing. Name, age, profession—I think people like to know that.'

Muriel paused and looked hopefully at them. 'What next?'

'Interests!' Alex told her. 'Although I'd steer clear of ones like "walks in the fresh air". Reading through some of them, you'd swear most of the women in the world were out walking in the fresh air.'

'Walking in the rain, perhaps?' Kenzie said, pen poised.

'Do you actually *like* walking in the rain?'

'I might if it was rain you see in English pictures, that just drifts mistily down and settles in shakeable drops on your coat, but our rain is like a deluge, taking all in its path. We don't call it the wet season for nothing, you know.'

* * *

He grinned at her and her bones did the melting thing again. This really was most peculiar. It wasn't as if she was attracted to the man! Not like she'd been to the dastardly Mark.

But even then, she was reasonably sure she hadn't felt internal agitation, neither had her wretched face flared like a beacon every time he'd teased her.

Maybe he hadn't ever teased her!

And even if she *was* attracted to Alex, she didn't want to be dilly-dallying around with a passing fling—not that she could imagine Alex as a 'fling' type of person—when she had to be concentrating on the marriage and children scenario.

'There must be some "how to" stuff about it on the internet. I'll check it on my phone,' Alex said.

'What's he doing?' Muriel asked, a little plaintively.

'Looking up how to write a good profile for a dating site. Not that he'll find anything, I'm sure.'

'Which just shows how much you know!' Alex said smugly. 'Look, there are dozens of sites about it, and even a template for writing your profile.'

'Ooh, I like the sound of a template. Then we just fill stuff in.'

Muriel was getting even more excited while Kenzie wondered why she'd ever mentioned the 'married and two children' business to these virtual strangers. They'd pushed her into it, though, with their talk about a bucket list.

And it *was* what she wanted—quite badly— so the words had just come out.

'What does it say?'

Muriel again, carried away by something new!

'Lists,' Alex replied. 'List of things you like. What do you like—something that might lead to a question.'

'You mean something along the lines of "I like walking in the rain. What's the rainiest walk you've ever had?" I'd be likely to land someone telling me about their stroll up Mount Everest only the rain turned to hail and then snow, and they'd been caught in an avalanche.'

'You're not taking this seriously,' Alex said severely. 'And here we are trying to help! What *do* you like?'

Kenzie gave up. They *were* trying to help her. At least Muriel was. She suspected for Dr A. McLeod it was just an amusing way to pass some time.

'Reading,' she said.

'That's good,' Muriel said warmly. 'Then you say what book it is you're reading now, and ask if he's read it.'

'The Iliad? I'd probably end up with some Greek scholar who wants to discuss the finer points of the Trojan Wars and I really don't know them. I'm only reading it because I'd read a book about the Trojan Wars written from the women's point of view—the women who became prizes of war and wives or slaves to the Greeks who conquered their cities.'

'You're reading the Iliad to get the male side of the war? Alex asked, in rather faint tones.

'Well, really to find out what happened from the male perspective but it was so mixed up with gods and legends that it didn't help. So I don't think I'd get on with someone who puts it down as his favourite book.'

'As if anyone is likely to!' Alex said. 'Did you really read it?'

She looked at him and grinned.

'Truthfully, no, not all of it. I just dipped in and out.'

His answering smile started the strangeness inside her again. She battled to think of other men she'd dated—not that she was dating Alex—but as far as she could remember, what there were of them had all been normal, sensible relationships with attraction there, certainly—but squirmy insides?

And hadn't she just decided that whatever he made her feel, it wasn't something she wanted to pursue? Neither did she need the distraction of these bizarre reactions to the wretched man.

Squirmy insides indeed!

From a smile?

'Wake up, Kenzie!'

Muriel snapped her out of her memories.

'Let's go down and eat,' she said. 'Alex, you might want to check on your grandmother first, and, Kenzie, I've found a skirt that would fit you. You can wear it with your black tank top. Shall we meet in the dining room?'

Kenzie opened her mouth to protest but realised it was futile, especially as Alex had left the room as soon as Muriel had suggested it. They were puppets on her string, but as it was giving her a great deal of pleasure, Kenzie went along with it.

The skirt was gorgeous, black silky material, with a riot of flowers like a garden around the bottom of it.

And being such a showpiece in itself, she felt she had to let it shine, pulling her hair severely back off her face and twisting it into a knot at the back of her head.

Damned if she wasn't beautiful!

That was Alex's first thought when he met them in the dining room—a little late as his grandmother had not only been awake but quite rational. They'd talked for ten minutes before she'd drifted off to sleep with a smile on her face after hearing stories of Muriel's horse-riding feats.

But seeing Kenzie!

It was a wonder the *Wow!* he'd thought hadn't burst from his lips.

He'd accepted she was attractive the first time he'd seen her, and the frank openness of her blue eyes when she'd spoken to him had certainly stirred something inside him.

But beautiful?

And now, right there in front of him, at the table by the window, was the woman he'd first associated with horses, looking so regally serene *and* so startlingly beautiful his breath caught in his throat and he had to pause to gather his senses.

And she was searching for love on the internet?

What was wrong with the men in her part of the world? And as for the fellow who'd led her on had hurt her...

He wasn't a violent man, but he wouldn't mind meeting *him* in a dark alley one night.

Because whoever it was *had* hurt her.

She might make light of it, saying this was nothing more than a little break to regroup, but he knew enough about gossip—he imagined small towns were like hospitals in that regard—to know how painful and humiliating that could be.

He pulled out his chair a little more forcibly than necessary and slid into his seat, careful not to look at Kenzie lest he have that breathing problem again.

She and Muriel were discussing the menu, Muriel encouraging Kenzie to try the little grilled octopi that were a specialty of the area, and Kenzie flatly refusing.

'I don't really like seafood, and I particularly don't like seafood with eyes. I'm having the steak because I happen to know it's the highest quality, imported from Australia.'

'Cattle have eyes,' Alex teased, because her cheeks had flushed as she'd argued with Muriel and he wanted to see that colour rise again.

'But not in the part I eat,' she said bluntly, glaring at him across the table, although that telltale colour *was* there again. 'Now, shall we talk about something else? Muriel would like to do one of the shorter mountain treks on her horse tomorrow, would you like to join us?'

The talk turned to horses and whether Muriel was really ready to be let off a leading rein—which she wasn't in his opinion but he doubted Muriel would listen to him, so determined was she to become a rider.

He would like to join them, very much so! If only to see Kenzie back in her jeans and T-shirt so he could get this evening's Kenzie out of his head.

'I'll have to see,' he said. 'My grandmother was more alert this evening than she's been for over a week and if she's like that tomorrow, I wouldn't want to leave her.'

'Of course not!' Kenzie said. 'But if you do come, you have a pager, I think you said, and could get back quite quickly to her room. We really won't go far.'

The waiter arrived at that moment to take their orders, which gave Alex time to consider whether he actually wanted to go on a short ride in the rainforest with Kenzie and Muriel.

Maybe not so much with Muriel…

Though having Muriel around was good because, much as he was attracted to Kenzie, he didn't want to get too involved with her. His life was on hold at the moment, so he could offer little more than a brief flirtation. And considering she'd just come out of a bad relationship, he certainly didn't want her to be hurt again.

He picked up his wine glass to taste the wine he must have ordered from another waiter who'd appeared by his chair, nodded his head and watched the waiter pour the women a glass each before adding more to his.

It was a very good shiraz, and the mellow liquid slid easily down his throat.

Giving him the courage to have another look

at Kenzie, as she sat, head cocked, listening to Muriel tell her about some riding gear she'd ordered through the boutique in the palace foyer.

Better by far that he leave the women on their own tomorrow, whether his grandmother was alert or not. It had been the talk of internet dating that had made him look at Kenzie in a different way.

Had to have been…

CHAPTER THREE

'ALEX'S GRANDMOTHER MUST be feeling well today,' Kenzie said, as she and Muriel climbed into a tuk-tuk to go down to the stables next morning.

What she didn't mention to Muriel was the relief she'd felt when he'd failed to appear at the arranged time.

Neatly be-suited for dinner in the formal dining room, he'd looked no different from the man they'd dined with the previous evening, yet something *had* been different about him. Something that was in the air between them—that had been there since he'd first appeared on the other side of the horse.

Or had she been imagining it?

Imagining that his teasing meant more than it did?

Imagining an attraction?

She shook her head. A practical, country-reared young woman, she'd had no time for the love-sick talk of the girls at boarding school. The 'Did you see how he looked at me?', 'Do you think he might like me?', Should I ask him to the dance?' conversations that were regularly heard after lights out in the dorms.

So, to be imagining there'd been something different in the air between them was completely foreign to her—a whole new concept.

Was it? she wondered. Hadn't she felt a tug of attraction to Mark when they'd first met?

She tried to remember, knew she'd liked him from the start, but more than that?

She shook her head.

He'd been amusing, fun to be with, and most of his attraction, she'd worked out later, had been his confidence in himself—his confidence that he could win any woman he wanted, although that hadn't led her far enough to go to bed with him.

Thank heavens!

But Mark was in the past and Alex was a very different man, unlike anyone she'd ever met.

Was it his difference that stirred something inside her?

Or maybe it was just the talk of internet dating and her nervous reaction to dipping her toe into that possibly murky water.

Whatever! She was glad he hadn't come. Glad because of the distraction he was causing her.

Kinda glad…

The trek into the fringe of the rainforest was highly successful, Muriel declaring she was ready to go further the following day, but Kenzie knew that, as a new rider, Muriel should rest the new muscles she'd been using.

'But the riding,' Muriel protested.

'You won't forget what you've learned in just one day off and it will be good for you to do something different.

'Now a shower and a massage for you,' Kenzie told her, when they returned to her room at the hotel.

'And you, what do you do now?' a deep voice asked, and Kenzie spun around to see a serious-faced Alex standing just outside.

'Oh, Kenzie's free until late afternoon, when she joins me for a drink,' Muriel volunteered. 'Do come in. Is there something she could do for you?'

The question was asked with the expectation

of an immediate answer, and Alex said politely, 'I thought we could have a chat.'

'Oh, yes?'

Kenzie hid an inward groan—no way was Alex going to get away with such a vague reply.

He looked from Muriel to Kenzie then back to Muriel and shrugged, holding out his arms in a helpless gesture.

Hesitating...

Pausing...

Not the cool, composed, tech-brilliant Alex they both knew.

'You're dithering!' Kenzie said to him, aware the words had a very accusatory tone.

He half smiled.

'So would you be!' he muttered, then he took a deep breath and they discovered what it was all about—the words blurted out as if he was afraid he might not get them finished if he lingered too long on them!

'You'll find out anyway,' he said, by way of a beginning. 'But my grandmother is conscious and quite alert and she's declared that her dying wish is to see me married. I've pointed out it's virtually impossible—small matters like a lack of a bride and international rules and regulations, but she's waved all that away.'

He paused, his face now tight with strain.

'She's spoken of it before—this wanting to see me married before she dies, and foolishly, I suppose, I've always assured her she'll still be around when I take the plunge.'

He looked away, through the window and out over the blue-green sea, thinking that he would have been married by now had his grandmother's health not deteriorated to the point where she hadn't long to live.

Not that he had any regrets about bringing her out here, which made him realise his relationship with Melanie had been wrong from the beginning. Something they had simply drifted into…

'And now she won't be—alive, that is—if I don't go along with her.'

He sounded so down-hearted Kenzie wanted to pat his hand, or put her arm around his shoulders, but she sensed he had more to say and probably needed to get it all out.

'I couldn't argue. She's got it all worked out, you see. Apparently, she doesn't think I'd have any trouble finding a bride.'

He sighed and turned back to Kenzie and Muriel.

'And much as I love my grandmother, and much as I realise this is emotional blackmail on her part, none of her suggestions for finding a bride seemed like a great idea.'

'I imagine it could get terribly complicated,' Kenzie said, trying to hide a smile at the image of a line of beautiful young women lining up at the palace.

'Oh, but—'

That was Muriel attempting to make a point, but Alex was already back in full flow.

'Then I remembered Kenzie saying that she wanted to get married, so I was going to ask her if she'd mind awfully marrying me. A purely business arrangement, of course.'

This to Muriel, not to the intended bride!

But it was Kenzie who picked up on his phrase.

'Marrying you?'

'Yes, I thought the idea might suit us both,' Alex said, as if this was a normal conversation between strangers. 'I need a bride and you want to get married—it's like a contract arrangement—a business decision.'

Kenzie closed her eyes, but it made no more sense when the world was dark so she opened them again.

'You mean marry you in some pseudo ceremony then call it quits later that day?'

He looked horrified.

'Oh, no! I couldn't cheat my grandmother like that! I mean really marry, at least for long enough—a year or two—to see if we suit. We'd have to try to make a go of it—to be fair to her. But, of course, it wouldn't have to be for ever.'

Kenzie bit back the *but she'll be dead* retort that jumped to her lips, and went for the last bit.

'Of course? Why *wouldn't* you want to be married to me for ever? Not that any of this was likely to happen but it was a bit rude to rule me out so flippantly.'

He looked a little stunned and she realised she'd reacted far too forcibly.

'No, no! I didn't mean it like that—just that it would be an arrangement to please my grandmother. She's been so good to me, and it would mean so much to her and—'

'Let's stop right there,' Kenzie said, realising she needed to slow down this avalanche of an idea before it swept them all away.

'*My* intention,' she reminded him, 'is to get married *and have kids*—two—and I can hardly do that if I'm tied up in some kind of pretend marriage with you, and that's if it's even possible for foreigners to marry here.'

'Oh, it is!' Alex said, latching onto the last bit—probably the easiest bit—with a beaming smile. 'My grandmother got Robert—he's her butler at home—but here he's more just someone who looks after her. Anyway, she got him to check and there's a priest on the island, and after we've done a bit of paperwork and presented it all to the *amphur*, the local registration office, the marriage would be legal anywhere.'

'There, you see!' Muriel put in, already, Kenzie guessed, planning a wedding in her head.

'But that's my point,' Kenzie protested. 'I want to get married to have children. Being tied up in a marriage could mean I can't get on with it for possibly years—who knows how long a divorce would take?'

She was aware she sounded slightly hysterical but to have this man—and Muriel—planning her future was like a crazy dream.

'I wouldn't mind about the children,' Alex said, all kind magnanimity. 'In fact, I think that's the whole idea of it. Gran wants me married so she knows the name will go on.'

'McLeod? But surely there are hundreds of thousands of McLeods all around the world.'

Alex grinned at her.

'Maybe tens of thousands, but it's not the McLeod that needs to be carried on but Monroe—her name. Different clan altogether.'

He paused, before adding, 'You wouldn't mind a Monroe thrown into the children's names, would you?'

Kenzie stared at the man. Perhaps she was dreaming. She looked around her—Muriel, Alex, beautiful tropical island—no, this was real.

Pull yourself together.

She straightened in her chair, and looked from Alex to Muriel—still making wedding arrangements in her head from the blank look in her eyes—then back to Alex.

'This is totally crazy,' she said firmly. 'You can't possibly be suggesting making this marriage real—having children with me just to please your grandmother.'

'It's her dying wish!' he said soberly, although she suspected he was finding her reaction to the whole situation enormously diverting. No doubt because she was becoming increasingly flustered by it!

'You're here on the island because it was her last wish to die in this place where she had her honeymoon. I don't think people are allowed to have more than one dying wish—or at least to call it that!'

Now he actually smiled.

'I imagine you can have as many as you like—after all, you're dying, so who's going to be petty enough to count?'

Floored by this logic, she glared at him.

'It still doesn't explain your apparent willingness to marry a woman you barely know, *and* have children with her, just to please your grandmother.'

'Well, the children aren't part of the deal with her, although I know that's why she wants me married. But I threw that in as a kind of bribe to get you to say yes.'

'Oh, I see!' Kenzie could feel anger rising inside her. Not good as she didn't think well when she was angry. 'And have you also sorted out where we'll live, as I believe cohabiting would be essential in order to produce my children?'

'Our children,' he said, sounding so smug that if Muriel hadn't been there she'd have slapped his face.

'They're *my* children—you don't have to have anything to do with them,' she snapped, aware somewhere in her brain that this was a nonsensical conversation.

He smiled and she had to sit on her hands to stop any violence.

'Oh, but aren't all children better off with two parents? Isn't that the prevailing view of the pundits of childhood.'

'I wouldn't know,' Kenzie spat at him through clenched teeth, 'but I do know I managed very well with just a father!'

At which stage she stood up and left the room. It was that or having a full-blown tantrum, which, she suspected, would delight Alexander Monroe McLeod, but might upset Muriel.

Down to the foyer and out through the front door, long strides putting her further and further from the totally ridiculous conversation in Muriel's room.

Maybe she'd imagined it!

Sunstroke?

She gave a huff of laughter at the ridiculous

idea—she who'd been born and bred in the tropics, spent long days moving cattle from one paddock to another under a blistering, midsummer sun—sunstroke was unlikely...

And much as she'd have liked to think she'd been dreaming, she knew full well she hadn't been. It had been that stupid talk of bucket lists that had started it, and she'd responded by denying the idea of a bucket list when her only plan was to get married and have two children.

Then Muriel had got caught up in the internet dating idea, and somehow Alexander Monroe McLeod had decided he only had to ask, she'd agree, and his grandmother would die happy.

Had he thought she was so desperate? Had she *sounded* desperate when she'd spoken of it?

True, she did want it, and would like to get settled sooner rather than later, so the children could grow up with their grandfather and absorb knowledge from him, as she had all her life.

And now she considered it a little more rationally, wouldn't this be better than picking up a virtual stranger on the internet?

Hadn't hundreds of women been cheated by people they'd met on the net?

And at least with Alex, she knew he wasn't after her money. He probably wasn't even aware she had money. Not many outsiders could translate cattle numbers and square kilometres of land into cold, hard cash…

Perhaps, just perhaps, it wasn't such a bad idea. And it wasn't as if a marriage of convenience was a new thing. Most of the larger properties in Australia had been built up through fortuitous marriages over many generations.

Heaven preserve me! Am I really thinking I might go ahead with this?

She felt a little flip deep inside her body and she didn't think it was dread.

It was definitely a physical reaction, and unlike anything she'd ever felt before.

But that could be because he was a stranger—practically—and meeting the man who'd invented DocSays was certainly special, so that could explain the flip.

Except it had felt like excitement.

Attraction?

That something she'd felt between them almost from the beginning?

Although while a little physical attraction might be okay—a definite plus from the children point of view—it wouldn't do to fall in love with the man.

This would be a purely business arrangement…

'What do you think?' Alex asked Muriel as he watched Kenzie storm out of the room as if all the furies in hell were after her.

'I think it's an excellent idea,' Muriel declared. 'At least you both know what you're getting—well, who you're getting—but what you're getting into as well. Alex, you need a wife, and Kenzie needs children—it's perfect!'

Stunned by this pronouncement, Alex decided silence was the best response, although now the children had been mentioned, his body had tightened at the thought of sex with Kenzie.

Muriel waited until she was sure she had his full attention, then said, 'Now the wedding! I know your grandmother doesn't need a great fuss, and I imagine that butler person you spoke of will support you, and, of course, I'll support Kenzie. But afterwards, when your grandmother retires to rest or sleep, we should have a nice dinner in the restaurant. And champagne—of course champagne. Possibly some at the wedding itself, if your grandmother is able to tolerate a small glass.'

Alex would have liked to protest. Since he'd begun to think about it, the idea of having Kenzie in his bed had sent tension spiralling through his body, and, in his mind, should they need food or champagne, there was always room service.

But he'd been around Muriel long enough to know that nothing short of a bulldozer would stop her once she was in planning mode. And maybe Kenzie would enjoy a small—short?—celebratory dinner.

As his mind drifted to the thought that maybe these marriages of convenience were a good idea—saved all that hassle of dating—Muriel brought him firmly back to the present.

'Have you something to wear?'

It took him a couple of minutes to process the question.

'I've a couple of suits.'

'You know there are tailors in the village who could run you up a dinner suit, or perhaps a morning suit, in a matter of days.'

She paused, frowning.

'Or a nicely tailored tropical suit. That would be good for meeting Kenzie's father as well.'

Alex eyed the woman who was arranging his life.

'I can't see myself in whatever a "tropical suit" might be and I don't think a morning suit would be a good idea, do you? It would just embarrass Kenzie—even a suit might be a bit much in the morning. I thought grey slacks and a white shirt, no tie—nice and casual.'

'Hmph!' Muriel said, her lips pursing in disapproval, but fortunately at that moment Kenzie walked in.

'All right, I'll do it,' she said, standing in front of him with just an edge of belligerence in her voice. 'I imagine you'll want it as soon as possible. What do I need? My passport, I presume? Anything else?'

'A statement that you're single,' Alex said, pushing down a new kind of excitement rising inside him and sticking to the purely practical. 'If your father could get someone official like a lawyer to fax that through, or scan it and send it by email, we can get it translated by an official here.'

She nodded before returning to the chair

she'd occupied earlier, about as far from where he and Muriel, who'd settled on the settee, as she could get.

'And I'm assuming a priest doing his thing will be sufficient for your grandmother? She's not going to want full bridal regalia and wedding cakes and things?'

Alex hid a smile and glanced towards Muriel, seeing from the tightening of her lips and downcast face she'd already been planning a wedding cake.

'No, no! The priest and the ceremony will be quite sufficient.'

Kenzie frowned at him for a moment.

'Then couldn't we just fake it?' she asked. 'Not with the real priest, of course, but have someone dressed up as a priest do the ceremony?'

He sensed this was a last desperate effort on her part to restore some normality to the situation. She didn't have to agree, of course, but he guessed the idea had more appeal to her than the internet dating had. As far as he could tell, she was a sensible, practical woman.

And she *did* want children!

So he couldn't resist teasing her with his answer to the 'faking it' suggestion.

'And cheat a dying woman?' he said smoothly.

Kenzie hung her head, and he could see the beautiful colour flushing up her neck and into her cheeks.

She really was something special, this woman he was about to marry...

'You're right of course. I shouldn't have suggested it again, but this is all so bizarre I don't know—it's not so much *what* to think but *how* to think about it.'

'You're worrying too much, making too much of it,' Muriel said quite sharply. 'It's a splendid idea because you both get what you want.'

She paused, adding in a softer tone, 'You'll have to work at it—the pair of you. Most people don't realise it, but marriage isn't easy. And a successful one takes work, a lot of work, although plenty of people don't bother.'

Kenzie stared at the woman she'd known for less than three weeks, and wondered just how long it had taken Muriel to realise the truth of her statement. That it *was* true, Kenzie didn't doubt for a moment! From what she'd worked out through conversations, Muriel had been married at least four times—maybe more...

Glancing from Muriel to the man who had so disrupted her morning—if not her life—Kenzie saw that he, too, was watching Muriel, and she guessed he, too, was wondering how long it had taken her to work out the advice she'd just passed on.

He was a handsome devil, this man she was going to marry—probably—and she took his distraction as an opportunity to really look at him. With his dark hair and tanned skin, his unusual grey eyes were quite startling, and, she feared, they saw far too much for all he often hooded them, so he seemed to be watching people with a slightly weary compassion.

Or was she just plain nuts? Had this marriage talk gone to her head and somehow turned rational thought to fancies?

Fancies of attraction?

No, that had been there from their first meeting—or some form of it.

But given that attraction, she had to be careful it didn't go too far—develop into something stronger. This was a purely practical arrangement so Alex would get a wife and she'd get the children she wanted. It would be stupid to mess it up with anything deeper.

Surely there'd be nothing worse than one-sided love…

Could she wear the sarong to the wedding?

The thought startled her.

Had she decided?

Had she actually said yes?

Of course she had! Mere minutes ago…

She closed her eyes and tried to clear her head, no longer certain where any of the nonsense stood.

'You'll need a dress.'

Muriel obviously had no doubts at all.

'*Not* a wedding dress,' Kenzie said, possibly just a little too loudly.

'Well, you don't want all your wedding pictures to have you standing there in a sarong, do you?'

'Wedding pictures?' Kenzie said faintly, then felt a firm hand on her shoulder.

Alex had crossed the room to stand beside her.

'Just relax,' he said, the pressure of his hand and the quiet words enormously reassuring.

'It's not as if we can get married today! There are a few papers and things to get organised, but…'

He paused and smiled down at her, which dismissed any idea of relaxing.

'I'm taking it from the discussion of clothes that you'll definitely go along with it?'

She felt her head move up and down. After all, she'd been considering marrying a man she met on the internet and had coffee with in a neighbouring town. At least she knew this man—well, had begun to know…

'Famous!' he said. 'It is such a favour to me I'll do everything I can to see you don't regret it! I'll get on with the arrangements and see you both at dinner.'

And with that, he was gone.

Aware he had, with unexpected help from Muriel, more or less bulldozed Kenzie into agreeing to marry him, he should probably be feeling at least a small amount of guilt, but no.

This woman he'd so fortuitously come across at the Palace of Peace and Contentment fascinated him, not only with her conversations about her home—an unimaginable place—but with her easy smiles and laughter, and the way she flushed so easily when he teased her.

In fact, if the sensation he was experiencing could be described in any way, he thought it might be excitement—together with a strangely satisfied warmth.

Setting aside the temptation of stirring warmth and excitement together in his mind, he returned to his grandmother's suite, where Robert, with his unflappable efficiency, had produced all the necessary documents, already translated into English, that the priest would require.

His grandmother was propped up on an array of pillows on the bed and sleeping, but a lighter sleep than the deep coma-like condition that had shadowed the previous weeks.

He smiled to himself.

She'd be relaxed—at ease—never for one moment doubting he'd do exactly as she'd requested, and never for a fraction of a moment considering such a request could have been difficult, or even impossible.

Thank heaven for Kenzie, a practical, sensible young woman with her own very definite reasons for wanting to get married. And he quite liked children and was ready to have his own—so that wasn't going to be a problem.

The wayward part of his mind that had been keen to connect warmth and excitement was now running off at a tangent about how soon they could be expected to begin—

No, think about the wedding.

What did he need to do?

Breeding told him he should speak to her father—maybe not to do the old 'asking for a hand in marriage' thing, but at least to introduce himself and explain why the hurry. She'd mentioned cattle in some staggering number so it would be a big place, and with the name Steele and the general idea it was in northern Australia, he began his search.

The extremely efficient internet provided him with more information than he'd ever considered possible. If it was the right Mr Steele, then he could understand why Kenzie wanted to have children. The property was vast and had been, as she'd said, in the same family for generations. The original Mr Steele, settling on what, from the pictures, looked like arid red desert, must have had his own doubts about it, to have named it 'Speculation'.

But from the parts Alex had read, it had turned out very well indeed, although he had no idea what this meant in terms of money, but they must be doing okay.

He checked the time difference, found it was four in the afternoon in northern Australia and phoned, reaching, after some switches from phone to phone, Mr Steele himself.

'Angus Steele,' the man said by way of introduction. 'Do I know you, Mr McLeod?'

'Not yet,' Alex told him, 'but I'm in Thailand, staying in the same hotel as your daughter. Everything is fine, there are no problems, but...'

He paused, totally lost as to where to go next.

'You want to marry her?'

The words were such a shock it took Alex a few moments to compute them.

'Well, yes,' he managed. 'She phoned you, sir?'

'I've just finished speaking to her,' the man said, 'and if she's happy with whatever arrangement you're making, then that's fine by me.'

There was a subtext to the words that even over the phone Alex could clearly hear. Something along the lines of *but if you hurt her I will kill you slowly and painfully and bury your body where it will never be found.*

Maybe not quite so murderous, but definitely a warning.

'I will take good care of her,' Alex said, and realised, as he said it that he wanted very much to take good care of the woman he was about to marry—this woman he barely knew!

He knew she'd been hurt by the bastard that had sent her fleeing here, and even thinking about that knotted his gut in a most uncomfortable way.

She was different—special—and he'd meant what he'd said, meant every word…

'See that you do,' Angus Steele said, confirming in words the subtext Alex had heard. 'I look forward to meeting you. Goodbye.'

Steele by name and steel by nature?

Not a subtle man, anyway, so probably not in the slightest bit concerned about a marriage of convenience.

It wasn't the fact that she'd thought he should be the first to know that had Kenzie phoning her father. It was more their closeness and wanting to share the knowledge that something big and important was about to happen in her life.

Because for all she'd tried to be practical about the strange proposal and the discussion that had followed it, it *was* a big and important thing in her life!

Brought up in a man's world, she'd had no sentimental feelings about wanting her father to give her away in a grand wedding ceremony. As far as they were both concerned, she and her father, she wasn't his to give away, but her own woman, making her own decisions about her life.

If there was one thing growing up on an isolated property taught you, it was independence because often all you had to rely on was yourself. True, at mustering time especially, there could be up to two dozen people on the property, a dozen residents most of the time, but if your horse shied at a snake and threw you down by the far dam, you needed to know which fence to follow home.

Would children growing up in Scotland, even for five years, be able to learn that knowledge, or should they make their home on the property from birth?

She shook her head—there were no children yet—and never would be if she didn't get her act together and work out what she was going to wear. And there they were again—the children! At some stage of their lives they'd want to see their parents' wedding photos, and she didn't want to be in a sarong...

Fortunately, before the children thoughts could go further, Muriel knocked on her door and came in with an armful of clothes, which she draped carefully on the bed.

'See if there's anything there that would suit you,' she said, and Kenzie smiled at her. Trust Muriel to be getting on with practical matters. 'And then tomorrow we could go down to the tailor in the village for any alterations.'

Muriel!

'You were going to rest,' Kenzie said, remembering her plans for the day.

Muriel waved a languid hand.

'Oh, I've decided I don't need that and Gan from down at the stables is going to bring my horse up here, and I'll get on at the side entrance where you showed me, and we'll do a little trek.'

She paused before adding, 'And I'll probably be late back for lunch so I phoned Alex and told him it might be a good time to introduce you to his grandmother—over lunch if she's alert enough to want any.'

'You did what?' Kenzie demanded, far too loudly, as the reality of the situation hit her like a fist. She was supposed to be the practical one in this relationship—the organiser—and she'd been dithering as her mind wandered down dead-end alleys about where her children— which she didn't and might never have—should live and their wanting—or not wanting—to look at her wedding photos...

'Sorry, Muriel, you're right, I have to meet her sometime.'

Muriel patted her arm in a soothing manner.

'That's all right, dear, all brides get a little uptight. I did before all my marriages, although you'd have thought I'd have got used to it. But every time I was so sure he was the right man—just showed how much I knew!'

Muriel departed for her ride with Gan, and Kenzie collapsed beside the pile of garments on the bed—most of which, she now realised, were elaborate evening gowns. Maybe she'd better visit the tailor down in the village who could produce a garment in twenty-four hours…

CHAPTER FOUR

KENZIE HAD BEGGED off dinner, claiming a headache, which Muriel appeared to find quite normal.

'Bridal nerves, dear,' she said. 'You order whatever you want and ask them to send it up, then have an early night.'

Going to bed at eight was certainly obeying those words, but sleep? How could sleep come when images of Alex and bridal gowns and children chased each other through her head? Even when she did sleep, well after she'd heard Muriel come in, the same apparitions danced through her dreams.

So Muriel bouncing into Kenzie's bedroom at what seemed like dawn but was actually close to nine, came as a literally rude awakening.

'I'm off for my ride,' Muriel announced. 'You make sure you go down to see the tailor, and don't worry about the cost. Whatever you decide will be my wedding gift to you.'

'But, Muriel, I haven't even tried on the dresses you've already left for me. There's sure to be something there that fits and looks okay.'

'Okay?' Muriel shrieked, in what Kenzie hoped was *mock* horror. 'You want to look better than *okay*! It's your wedding, remember!'

Only too well, Kenzie thought but didn't say. She promised Muriel she'd visit the tailor and, yes, she'd remember she was having lunch with Alex and his grandmother, although what she really felt like doing was pulling the sheet over her head and going back to sleep. She dragged herself out of bed, showered and dressed, slapped her hat on her head and set off down to the village.

Where she not only found the miracle tailor, but the man she was going to marry, standing very still in the middle of a very small hut, having lethal-looking pins stuck into whatever it was he was wearing.

Inside out!

'Wedding finery?' she teased, hoping the little tingle along her nerves hadn't generated the blushes that came too easily. But even in an inside-out garment stuck with pins, the man was decidedly handsome—and, yes, it *had* to be attraction she kept feeling, which, all things considered, was probably a good thing…

'Gran!' he said succinctly, and her smile widened as she heard the name that had obviously clung on from childhood, on his lips.

'And you? Muriel?'

'Of course,' Kenzie said. 'Her argument was that I needed to think about the wedding photos.'

'Wedding photos?' Alex echoed faintly, wincing as a wayward pin struck skin.

'Exactly!' Kenzie said, 'but I could hardly tell Muriel there wouldn't be any wedding photos, now, could I?'

He said nothing, though the hint of a smile quirked one corner of his lips.

'Gran—who has apparently decided it's not time for her to die after all—simply pointed out that you'd probably be disappointed if I turned up in a white shirt and grey slacks.'

He paused, smile gone and eyes thoughtful.

'Although photos would be a good idea. You'll want to send some to your father, surely.'

And for some unfathomable reason Kenzie felt tears welling in her eyes.

Had Alex seen them that he stepped forward, pins and all, to put his hand on her shoulder?

She rubbed the overflow off her cheeks, startled by her reaction.

'I'm not at all sentimental, you know,' she muttered.

'Of course you're not,' he said, getting as close as the danger of the pins permitted and sliding his arm around her shoulders. 'Would you like him to be here?' he asked. 'I could have him flown over—it's no distance.'

Kenzie shook her head. As if her father *wouldn't* have been here if they weren't in the middle of mustering. She looked up at the man being so kind.

'I'm all right,' she said. 'I don't know why I went weepy on you, but I promise I won't do it again.'

To his surprise, the statement disappointed Alex, who'd found himself enjoying even this most ordinary of physical contact with Kenzie.

Had he been looking for an excuse to touch her?

Hold her?

If only to comfort...

He shook his head and stepped back for the tailor to fit more pins.

Not consciously, he hadn't—he was fairly certain about that, but he had to admit that ever since the marriage idea had raised its head the part of his brain not overseen by reason had been playing with any manner of thoughts.

And images, if he was honest!

'Well, I should be nearly done,' he said, when he realised the silence between them was growing heavier by the minute. 'Then it will be your turn.'

She'd stepped back from him as well, so the distance was now quite safe, but he sensed that the confusion he read in her eyes was nothing to do with an absent father but more along the lines of what he'd been thinking himself.

Well, as Muriel had said, they were both young—fairly young for him—healthy adults so why shouldn't there be an attraction between them?

He felt his body stirring and asked the tailor—a little too abruptly—if he was finished.

'Nearly,' the man told him, just as a woman appeared and led Kenzie into a tiny, curtained alcove in a corner of the shop.

He *would not* think about Kenzie stripping off her clothes behind that flimsy bit of cloth. He'd think about fish, or what to order for lunch—probably the latter because thinking about fish made no sense at all.

Not that anything was making much sense when Kenzie was around. It had to be the wedding business because generally sense— common sense—was one of his best attributes.

Or so he'd always thought...

He eased out of the pale cream, Thai-style shirt the tailor was making for him, called a cheery goodbye towards the curtain and left, glad to be out in the sunshine among the milling market crowd, glad to be heading back to the hotel and, he hoped, some sanity.

He was on the very edge of the crowd when he heard a shrill scream from somewhere behind him, and turned, thinking it was probably some over-excited child. But it was followed by another, and a lot of excited chatter.

Reluctantly he headed back into the market, the noise now persistent enough for him to know where he was going. The crowd had formed a circle around a heavily pregnant woman who lay writhing on the ground, her baby clearly on the way. Alex pushed his way through and knelt by the woman's side, wiping her hair out of her eyes, feeling the sweat on her face.

'Has someone called an ambulance?' he asked, aware that many of the locals would speak English and should understand the request.

No reply.

He knelt beside her, and gently asked her name.

'Malee,' someone from the crowd replied.

'I'm Alex,' he told her, 'and I'm a doctor,' thinking this might comfort her while at the same time wondering whether he could examine her more intimately in front of so many people.

Then another figure crupted from the crowd. Kenzie!

'Get back, get back, give her some privacy!' she yelled as she ran towards the woman, dropping to kneel beside her. 'Find a sheet and some towels, get something to cover her and something clean for the baby.'

This directed to a woman who'd tentatively followed her onto centre stage.

And as if by magic, lengths of material appeared, and bath towels still wrapped in plastic.

'Get a couple of the women to hold those up. The poor woman doesn't want the whole village watching her give birth,' Kenzie said to him.

'Malee, her name's Malee,' he said but Kenzie was already lifting the woman's knees into a position where she could check the cervix for dilatation.

Thankful for her presence, Alex organised the privacy screens, and sent someone to get water, and ice if it was available.

As quickly as the towels had appeared, water and ice arrived, and he knelt by the woman and cradled her head and shoulders, so she could sip at the cold water between pains.

'You'll be all right, Malee,' he said gently. 'You and the baby!'

Her hands gripped his supporting arms, fingers digging into them like talons.

'Head's crowned,' Kenzie said, glancing up at him briefly. 'I don't suppose you know the Thai word for push?'

But words weren't necessary. The woman screamed again, her fingers gripped the muscles on his arms so tightly he wondered if he'd end up scarred for life by this pre-wedding experience.

The baby arrived to a shout of joy from Kenzie, a sigh from Malee, and two ambulance attendants who took in the scene at one glance and immediately began to get both woman and baby into the ambulance.

Alex smiled to himself as he saw the reluctance with which Kenzie handed over the tiny, towel-wrapped infant.

'You wanted to keep holding it, didn't you?' he teased, as he took her by the elbow and forced their way through the still chattering crowds.

'Him,' Kenzie said, 'and I did not!'

She smiled. 'But it's always like a miracle, delivering a baby. There's something so...precious somehow about the perfection of it all.'

'You've had midwifery training?'

They were free of the crowds now, heading up the hill towards the hotel.

'Of course! There's not much point working in a country hospital if you can't deliver a baby.'

He slid his arm around her shoulders and gave her a hug.

'You did well,' he said, and though she tried

to shrug off the compliment, he saw faint colour in her cheeks and knew she'd liked it.

They met up with Muriel when they reached the stables. She took one look at Kenzie and rushed towards her.

'What happened? Are you all right? There's blood on you.'

Kenzie moved out of the shelter of his arm, leaving a coldness down his side.

She grinned at her excitable friend.

'It's not my blood, it's the baby's—or more probably Malee's, the mother's—but it's definitely not mine. We just delivered a baby, Alex and I, down by the markets. Oh, damn!'

'What's wrong?' Alex asked her, a spurt of worry in his gut.

'I left my hat and shoulder bag down there at the tailor's. I'll have to go back.'

He caught her hand as she turned.

'I'll go,' he said. 'You go in and get cleaned up.'

'So I don't shock your grandmother looking like this?' she teased, holding out her hands and gesturing to the murky stains.

'Just go,' he said firmly, hoping his voice was steadier than his heart, which had reacted most erratically to the sight of her more or less offering herself to him, though, of course, she wasn't doing that at all, It had been a quirk of his imagination and...

Well, he didn't know 'and what', but he'd better stop thinking about it and get her things as quickly as possible so he'd be back in time for lunch.

A pleasant buzz, the result of having helped deliver a healthy baby, stayed with Kenzie as she showered and dressed in a demure yellow sun frock that her father always loved to see her wearing.

Would Alex's gran approve?

She found herself hoping the old lady would, as if the sensible business arrangement of this marriage had turned into something else.

Not that it had.

True, Alex had taken her elbow to get her through the crowd, but once they'd been through and out on the road to the hotel, he'd dropped it.

There'd been no reason for him to keep holding it, or for her to have expected it of him, but that temporary closeness had suggested togetherness, and wasn't that what marriage was all about?

These rambling thoughts chased through her head as she swiped on some pale pink lipstick and smoothed down the wildness of her hair, braiding it into a neat French plait.

Well, most of it. Those shorter bits that curled close to her face always did their own thing, and she didn't want to meet Alex's grandmother smelling of hairspray, which never held them for long anyway.

Satisfied that she was done, she went into the living room and did a twirl for Muriel, who told her she looked beautiful, and she hoped Alex realised just what a gem he was getting.

'You're looking good yourself,' Kenzie replied. 'All this horse-riding out in the fresh air obviously suits you.'

'I just love it!' Muriel said, her face aglow with remembered delight. 'I'm going out again this afternoon. Gan knows a little beach that's very private. He says the horses like walking in the water. Imagine that, Kenzie, me on a horse in the water!'

Kenzie smiled at her.

'Wish me luck!' she said, as she gave the

woman who'd become a friend a quick kiss on the cheek.

'As if you need luck!' Muriel said. 'It's that Alex getting the luck, with you agreeing to marry him. Gan says—'

But before Kenzie could learn what Gan had said, the sweet chime of the bell at the entrance to the suite told her Alex was here, ready, as he'd promised, to escort her up to the penthouse.

She greeted him a little distractedly, brushed aside his compliment on how she looked, and frowned back at the door she'd just closed behind her.

'Are you worried about leaving Muriel on her own?' Alex asked. 'You must get some time to yourself, surely.'

Kenzie shook her head.

'No, no! She's the most generous of employers and we get on really well.'

'But?' he probed, and again she shook her head.

'It's nothing and even if it is, then it's not my business, and certainly not something I could discuss with a stranger.'

His lips quirked into a wry smile.

'Am I still a stranger?'

The question brushed away the niggle of concern she'd felt earlier, and she considered it for a moment.

'Well, we're not exactly old friends, are we?'

CHAPTER FIVE

MRS MONROE—GRAN—proved to be a formidable woman, for all she was withered by age and propped on pillows in the most luxurious bed Kenzie had ever seen.

In the most luxurious room ditto!

A golden room that seemed to glow with sunlight, although the effect, Kenzie was pretty sure, came from the fine silk of the golden curtains that hung at the windows and formed a canopy over the old four-poster bed.

Here and there, silver touches, like the material covering the sofa, seemed to enliven the gold, while bright pink and green cushions provided, surprisingly enough, a pleasing contrast.

It was impossible not to compare it to the—well, drab furnishings of her own home. 'Home' on a cattle property was a totally utilitarian place, brown and grey the predominant colouring in the furnishings—practical colours out in the red desert country.

Perhaps if her mother had lived…

She felt a sudden surge of emotion, as strong as it was unexpected, and for a moment she longed for the mother she'd never known. She shut her eyes against tears, and shook her head to clear it, determined to get with the conversation.

'Gran was asking how you're enjoying your stay.'

'I'm sorry, Mrs Monroe—this room just took my breath away.'

The old lady smiled, and Kenzie saw in the sweetness of that smile how beautiful Gran had once been. The high cheekbones beneath her grey, sagging skin still commanded attention, as did her deep blue eyes, for all they were clouded by age.

'Alexander's mother was conceived in this bed.'

Why hadn't Alex warned her that his gran was a woman who spoke her mind?

It had been a statement of fact, apparently, and not something Kenzie could easily answer.

But she was here to impress, so she did her best.

'That must make it extra-special that you've been able to return with him,' she said.

'Return to die!'

It was another conversation stopper, but fortunately Alex came to her rescue, suggesting they order lunch.

'Gran has hers in a tray in her bed, but Robert has set up a small table for us close by.'

He waved his hand towards a small, round table, a snowy white tablecloth forming a backdrop to a vase of pale pink roses. Silver cutlery was set out in front of two chairs, both angled so anyone sitting there could see and be seen by the old woman.

'Alexander tells me your mother died in childbirth. That must have been hard on you, growing up without her.'

The words were weak and slow, but Kenzie sensed her interest.

'I have never known anything different,' she answered quietly. 'It has always been me and my father, although other people were around. My mother's mother lived with us when I was a baby, and we had two couples living on the property, and the women were always there for me.'

'Cattle, I think Alexander said?'

'Yes, Brahmans. They do best in the tropical conditions, they're fairly drought resistant and don't attract ticks.'

The old lady did not respond and Kenzie was thankful when Robert appeared, carrying a silver tray. He unfolded small legs on either side of it and set it over Mrs Monroe. Robert then placed a plate in front of each of them and a platter of meats, salad vegetables and exotic fruits in the middle of the table.

Mrs Monroe—far better to think of her as that, rather than the way too intimate Gran—was sipping from a tall glass of some indeterminate concoction that had a look of one of the green health juices that had become so popular. Anything, Kenzie guessed, to get fluids into her without tethering her to the unsightly paraphernalia of a drip.

Kenzie helped herself to meat and salad, her selection making barely a dint in the mass of food in front of them.

But her nerves were tightening and too many doubts were flashing through her mind. Should she ask questions of Mrs Monroe while she was drinking her juice? Or not speak at all?

She could ask about the juice, but that might prove too personal if it turned out it was purely medicinal…

Moving her food around her plate and becoming increasingly distracted, she finally looked up and glared at Alex, who was watching her with that damn smile in his eyes.

She frowned at him, hoping he'd pick up the conversational ball, but he was obviously enjoying her discomfort far too much to end it.

Talk about a bedroom farce!

'Is it medicinal, your juice?' Kenzie finally asked, and Mrs Monroe placed the glass on the silver tray and said, 'No, but Robert tells me it's very healthy.'

She paused, and Kenzie waited, hoping she had more to say, or that Alex might join in, but that was not to be. Silence once more settled like a shroud in the room.

Well, here goes!

'My father drinks a weird concoction that has beetroot in it, making it a vivid purple. He had severe arthritis in his hands and fingers and made the decision years ago to give up all the nightshade vegetables—potatoes, tomatoes, eggplant and capsicum. He claims it cured him, and his hands really are proof of it. Sweet potatoes are okay, apparently, and he loves his beetroot. Our gardener grows them especially for him.'

A muffled snort from across the table told her just how much the man she'd thought she might marry was enjoying this, but the silence increased the tension of her nerves, so if she had to chatter on, she damn well would.

Another glare across the table produced nothing but a bland smile.

She eyed the plate in front of her. No way could she eat anything. Her stomach was in knots, so it was with huge relief she heard Mrs Monroe's weak, tired voice.

Relief until she heard exactly what was being said.

'I think she'll do very well indeed, Alexander,' the old woman said, then she waved her hand, apparently dismissing them both, for Robert came forward to lift her tray from the bed, and she lay back in her pillows and cushions and closed her eyes.

Aware she was probably scarlet with embarrassment, Kenzie scrambled to her feet, murmured something she hoped would be taken as a thank you and farewell, and prepared to depart.

Needing to be out of the room, out of the hotel, anywhere in the fresh air where she could work out exactly what she needed to say to Alexander Monroe McLeod.

But he caught her hand as she passed him, and held it while he stood up, murmuring, 'You've eaten nothing. Come on and I'll take you down to the village for something hot and spicy.'

'I would prefer to be alone!' she said with as much hauteur as she could muster.

'Because I laughed?' he teased.

Fortunately, they were outside the suite by now, so she could turn to him and tell him exactly what she thought of him.

'You did that on purpose—left all the conversation to me. You didn't help one bit, and I ended up rabbiting on about beetroot, of all things! You could have helped, asked questions even, done something rather than sitting there enjoying every minute of the torment!'

He grinned at her.

'It was far too good to interrupt. Besides which, you will have impressed Gran no end. She believes people should all contribute something to the conversation.'

'*You* didn't!' Kenzie snapped, then realised he was still holding her hand.

And, worse, she'd done nothing about removing hers from his grasp.

And neither did she particularly feel like doing it.

Weird!

She caught up with his conversation, something about his grandmother loving him anyway, so he hadn't had to talk.

She'd remove her hand when they reached the lift, she decided.

Definitely before they walked out of it into the foyer...

But somehow, here she was, halfway down the drive, the hat he'd rescued earlier pulled down on her head, her handbag slung across her shoulder, and her hand still in his.

Well, they *were* getting married so maybe it was okay to hold hands with him—even if he was a stranger...

* * *

Alex felt a sense of enormous satisfaction as he walked, hand in hand, with this attractive woman.

There'd been women in his life, some passing through it, others more serious, but none had held his heart for very long. In fact, few had ever *touched* his heart, not the way he imagined his parents' hearts had been touched by each other.

He knew his focus on work had destroyed many of his relationships, but he'd sometimes wondered if there was something lacking in him, or if, perhaps, their early deaths had coloured his world too much. Had raised his expectations too high...

His memories of them from before the light plane crash in the highlands had claimed their lives had been of two people who had somehow become one. He'd seen their eyes meeting across a formal dining table, drawing small, secretive smiles from both of them. Seen how the casual touch of his father's hand on his mother's shoulder could draw colour into her face and a special light into her eyes.

They'd worked and lived and laughed their

way through life, making everything around them seem brighter—more alive, more vibrant somehow...

But maybe the judgement of a twelve-year-old boy wasn't all that reliable.

And maybe what they'd had had been special, and his own failure in the love department was because he was looking for that magic he'd once seen, and even felt—for their love had wrapped around him as well.

They'd been in the highlands with Gran for his holidays, and he'd been staying on.

Gran's recipe for heartbreak and grief, though he hadn't known at the time, was to keep busy all the time.

They'd collected butterflies and heartlessly pinned them into a collector's display case, learned their names from heavy books in her grand library, patiently typed them out on her ancient typewriter...

Gran's ghillie, McNab, had taught him to shoot, for all his father had once said he had to wait until he was fourteen. Targets first—great round things that he could hardly miss, then cans on fence posts, more the size of vermin!

And with McNab and Gran and a picnic basket stuffed with goodies, they'd drive the small pony cart to the open land beyond the forest to shoot at the rabbits that ate the local farmers' crops.

And every day, even if only for an hour, he rode the big black gelding that had been his grandfather's horse. Exercising him, Gran said, though looking back Alex wondered if she'd asked him to do it because riding Duke needed all your concentration, so even on these jaunts high up into the hills, he'd had little time to feel sad.

He'd felt loss—*that* lived with him—lived as a shadow he doubted would ever leave, but he was kept too busy to wallow in abject misery. Besides which, as Gran had said one day when she'd found him crying, 'Monroes don't do emotion! It's just not done...'

Lost in the past, he was surprised to find they'd reached the market, where excited voices greeted them, obviously regarding them—or at least Kenzie—as the heroes of the hour after the delivery of the baby. The crush of people pressed Kenzie closer to him, and he felt the softness of her body. He dropped the hand he'd somehow been holding to put his arm around her shoulders.

For protection from the crush, of course...

No, admit it, he liked touching her, had liked holding hands and even more feeling her body close to his.

And best of all, it was a sensible, business arrangement, so he didn't have to worry if that spark of magic he'd seen within his parents' marriage didn't happen to him.

'What do you fancy?' he asked, and was pleased when she responded promptly.

'The satay chicken on sticks,' she said without a moment's hesitation. 'The ones you get at the place with the yellow umbrellas at the edge of the market, right near the beach.'

Not that he'd expected quite that much precision, but at least she hadn't said, 'Oh, I don't know, what are you having?' which was the answer most women he had known would have given.

He eased them through the crowd to the stall she'd mentioned, ordered the same for both of them, added some sparkling mineral water to the order, then joined her at a table right on the sand.

She'd kicked off her sandals and was flicking at the sand with her toes. Small, pink toes, unadorned by any hue of nail polish, but perfect nonetheless.

Perfect toes?

Was he losing his mind?

Maybe it was just that he wasn't used to seeing naked toes that hers seemed so...right?

But sitting there, seeing those toes flicking sand into little arcs in the air, he felt a sense of well-being and knew it stemmed from the woman by his side.

Knew it stemmed from the attraction he felt—not just for her toes but for the whole, beautiful package, who laughed and joked and smiled a lot and quite simply made him feel good.

Although it was probably a good thing that he was physically attracted to her—something he'd only just got around to admitting to himself—given that she wanted children.

'So,' she said, using a napkin to wipe a smear of satay sauce from the corner of her upper lip, 'when's the big day?'

'Big day?' he found himself echoing, as his attention was diverted away from that upper

lip. He could have licked that sauce off it—
that's what he'd *been* thinking.

'The wedding,' Kenzie said, an unspoken
'stupid' lingering at the end of the two words.

He studied her now, wondering if she was as
laid-back about all this as she seemed.

If he gave himself a slap on the cheek to get
his mind into gear, would she think he was de-
mented and back away from the arrangement
as fast as her pretty feet would allow?

He closed his eyes and breathed deeply instead, aware that the gap between her question
and his reply was lengthening by the second.

'I think Robert said tomorrow,' he finally
managed. 'Would that suit you?'

'Of course!' came the answer, far too cool and
off-hand. Maybe she *was* as laid-back as she
seemed. Maybe it was an Australian thing...

Tomorrow?

She was getting married *tomorrow*?

Good thing this was a business arrangement,
because she wasn't feeling the slightest hint of
excitement!

Shouldn't she be?

Feeling something, at least?

But, no, a quick mental scan of organs found nothing untoward.

Perhaps not surprising when it was a purely business arrangement, something that suited them both…

Although if she gave any thought to after the wedding—in fact, the wedding night—well, that was different.

Even this quick reminder of it had set her nerves jangling, her stomach tightening, and heat sweeping up through her body, about to betray her with a blush.

'Thank heavens for the hat!'

And it was only when Alex echoed her words—'Thank heavens for the hat?'—that she realised she'd spoken aloud.

'I'd be getting a sunburnt nose without it,' she said, pleased with herself for being so calm.

'You might have already caught a bit of the sun, even with the hat,' he said, smiling at her as if he knew full well that she was blushing.

'Then perhaps we should head back,' she said firmly, refusing to acknowledge his tease.

'Well, I have to call at the tailor,' he said. 'Will you walk that way with me or go up on your own?'

'The tailor—I'd forgotten all about her. Mine's a woman, I think the wife. I'll come with you, although they'll probably want me to try it on to see if it fits so I could be a while. You should go on ahead.'

He smiled at her, something she was beginning to wish he wouldn't do because it was very hard for her to maintain her cool composure when he did.

'Don't want me seeing you in your wedding dress before the big day,' he teased, totally destroying any cool at all.

'It's not a wedding dress and it's hardly that kind of wedding day,' she snapped.

And the infuriating man smiled again.

But they did visit the tailor together, Alex collecting his shirt in a plastic bag while Kenzie, as she'd supposed, was ushered behind the flimsy curtain.

'You go on ahead,' she said to Alex. 'I could be ages and your grandmother might need you.'

He hesitated, and for a moment she thought he was going to offer to wait, but in the end he gave her a nod and walked away—much to her relief.

It had to be the imminence of the wedding that had rattled her nerves on the beach.

Was she sure about this?

Of course not, because that was just a sensible arrangement.

No, it had been thinking of the after-wedding scenario that had sent blood thrumming through her veins.

She had to forget that and concentrate on practicalities!

Being married and having two kids was definitely the goal, and when Alex had suggested it, the idea had made sense. A nice, clean, business kind of arrangement that would suit them both.

Then why was she so uptight?

Had it been the hand-holding thing?

At first she'd welcomed his hand taking hers after the ordeal of lunch with Gran, but then to keep hold of it—for her to let him—well, it had seemed strange somehow—but nice strange...

Which was where her confusion lay...

Although wasn't it good that she'd felt comfortable holding his hand? Given the children idea, they were going to do much more intimate things than that.

And there it was again, the excited little flip in her chest, the beat of her heart sounding in her ears.

And here came that wretched blush again!

How had she never grown out of it, as all her friends had?

Her mother hadn't been a blusher—she'd checked that out with various people who'd known her.

So why her?

She sighed, and slid into the calf-length cream slip of a dress the tailor held over her head.

Studied the Kenzie in the mirror.

Could one dress really make that much difference?

She turned slowly, feeling the silk sliding over her skin—

'It's perfect,' she said to the beaming woman, although now her stomach was knotting in case it looked too much like a wedding dress.

Well, it *was* a wedding dress—not beaded with crystals or layered with appliqué—no train, no veil, just a simple cream Thai silk sheath.

And she felt beautiful in it.

'Thank you so much,' she said to the woman,

taking her hands and pressing them softly to emphasise her delight.

'It was my pleasure,' the woman said, 'to dress so beautiful a bride.'

But when Kenzie went to pay, she was told Alex had already covered the cost, and the annoyance he could so easily arouse in her steamed to the surface.

How dared he?

Did he think she wouldn't be able to afford it?

That she was marrying him for his money?

Though dimly aware that she was building mountains out of molehills, she continued to feel aggravated by his behaviour.

Demanding to know how much he had paid, she thanked the woman once again and headed for the nearest cash machine, withdrawing not only enough to pay him back but enough to cover any other expenses that might arise.

With the dress in its plastic bag, folded carefully over her arm, she made her way through the market, pausing by a lingerie stall that seemed to sell nothing but very erotic nightwear in bright blue, purple or red.

But she'd lingered too long. A small girl who

should surely have been at school had sidled up to her.

'Things for you are inside, lady,' she whispered, guiding Kenzie towards a small door and waving her hand towards a display of beautiful lingerie. Filmy silk now, not the slub silk of her wedding gown but beautifully embroidered nightdresses, some with matching negligées.

Well, why not have something special—something a bit more seductive than her short, almost threadbare cotton nightshirt with the kangaroo on the front of it?

She bought three of the lovely nightgowns but restricted herself to one negligée, then wondered if she'd ever wear any of them.

Of course she would, she assured herself, but with every passing moment the reality of what she was doing became less and less believable—kind of foggy and far off, not looming like the word 'tomorrow' had suggested.

CHAPTER SIX

THE SOFT CHIME of the doorbell wakened Kenzie, and she leapt up from the sofa where she'd fallen asleep, the book she'd been reading now lying on the floor.

Muriel was dining with some friends who'd just arrived, and having had the chicken on the beach, Kenzie had stayed in the suite, picking up the book to stop herself thinking about what lay ahead, especially with nerve endings tingling beneath her skin and her brain tossing what-ifs at her.

Tomorrow.

She opened the door to find the man she didn't want to think about standing there.

'I saw Muriel at dinner and thought this might be a good opportunity to talk about some practicalities.'

'Practicalities?' Kenzie echoed, still fuzzy from her short sleep.

He smiled at her.

'Business matters,' he said. 'Do you think I might come in?'

Suddenly aware they were still in the doorway, she stepped back to let him enter and shut the door behind him.

'Business matters?'

Damn and blast, she was behaving like a moron, repeating everything he said.

'It's a business arrangement,' he reminded her, but gently, touching her lightly on the shoulder and guiding her back to where she'd been sitting.

She still couldn't get her head around it, her mind now considering the warm patch on her shoulder where his hand had rested.

'Are you contracted to Muriel or the hotel? I need to speak to someone about that.'

Contract? Come on, Kenzie, get with it here! Of course you have a contract.

'I answered an ad for a nurse/companion the hotel put online, but it was specifically for Muriel. She'd arrived here and hadn't liked whoever was available for her, so the ad wanted someone who could start immediately, and immediately if not sooner was what I wanted.'

'So, I'll talk to the hotel about it.'

Was it that small sleep she'd had that made this sound confused?

And had she had confusion written clearly on her face that he took her hand and said, 'Kenzie, we'll be married. The big bonus for me, right now, is that I'll have some company. I've been bored out of my skull these last few weeks.'

'So you'll tell the hotel I'm working for you, not Muriel?'

He shook his head.

'You'll be *living* with me, not Muriel!'

And before she could make even a feeble protest—*or* allow herself to think about that statement, he added, 'How else can we get on with providing you with children.'

'But Muriel. I'll be letting her down. I thought we'd get married for your gran then go on as before. I can't just walk away from Muriel!'

He took her other hand and held them both captive in his.

And smiled, which was her undoing, for the meaning of his words about the children finally dawned on her and she could feel that wretched heat searing her cheeks.

He touched a finger to her cheek.

'I love the way you blush. My mother used to—she hated it—but sometimes one look from my father was enough for the lovely rosiness to colour her cheeks.'

Hmph! There really wasn't anything she could say to that! Except...

'To get back to Muriel,' she said, 'I already know there's no one on staff she wanted for a companion, so I'd be letting her down. Couldn't we, you know—couldn't I—'

'Couldn't we sleep together in Gran's suite and you come bouncing down to play with Muriel during the day?'

Kenzie nodded.

'No!' he said, and just when she thought that was it—just no, he continued, 'It wouldn't be right. Besides which I've already spoken to Muriel about it—I'm the "friends" she had dinner with tonight. She's more than happy for you to move up to the penthouse with me. In fact, it was she who suggested I come and see you now, so you can pack your things to have sent up tomorrow. She's quite happily reading to Gran as we speak.'

Kenzie could only stare at him. Maybe it was the speed at which this was all happening that was boggling her mind, but, whatever it was, she found it impossible to frame a sensible sentence—let alone an objection to his high-handed ways.

Alex could almost read the thoughts flitting through her head. Who was he to be making all these arrangements? That was probably the foremost of them, for he already knew—or guessed—enough about her to know she was fiercely independent.

No doubt as a result of being brought up in an isolated area...

While the kindness he'd seen and sensed in her—who else would have ploughed on so valiantly in that conversation with Gran?—would have her worrying about Muriel.

'Muriel will be fine,' he said gently. 'In fact, I think Muriel has already made alternate arrangements, and while she'll miss having you at her beck and call all the time, you've more than done your duty, teaching her to ride.'

His bride-to-be looked up at this, and smiled.

'Can you imagine how empty her life must have been that she's embraced it so enthusiastically?'

He squeezed her fingers and admitted, 'Actually, I can. It wasn't until I came out here that I realised I'd filled my life with work—to the exclusion of everything else. And when I didn't have work I found I had nothing. It's made me realise a lot of things about myself—some of them not very positive,'

And still holding her hand in one of his, he slipped his arm around her shoulders and drew her closer.

'At least meeting you and Muriel put a stop to that,' he said, wondering if, with her lips so close, he should kiss her.

Or was intimacy, in a business marriage, something that should be discussed first?

Having no answer to that inner question, he kissed her cheek, and felt a shiver of reaction run through the body pressed to his.

She eased away, slowly enough to make it clear it wasn't a reaction to the chaste kiss, but apparently to study him, for she sat, still close, and looked at his face, her head tilted slightly as if that made it easier for her to take him in.

He half smiled, and she smiled back.

'It's just a bit weird, isn't it?' she said.

His own smile grew.

'More than a bit,' he said. 'Far more than a bit.'

She continued her survey for a few seconds more, then leaned over and kissed *his* cheek.

'Muriel's probably tired of reading now,' she said. 'And I need to pack.'

She stood up and he joined her, still holding her hand.

'Goodnight kiss?' he suggested, in part, at least, to see her cheeks colour up again.

Which they did, and seeing her so flushed and lovely, blue eyes wary but excitement there as well, how could he not kiss her?

A quick kiss on her lips—a butterfly kiss—because deep inside him he had become aware that once he kissed this woman properly, it was unlikely he'd want to stop.

The day finally dawned, Kenzie greeted by a huge bouquet of Australian native flowers, although how a local florist could have sourced such blooms, she had no idea.

She didn't have to look at the card to know they were from her father. 'For you, darling girl, from all of us on Spec,' the card read, and

Kenzie closed her eyes against her tears and pictured everyone at home, gathering, as she was sure they would—mustering or not—to celebrate her wedding.

The maid who'd delivered them to Muriel's suite went off to find vases, while Kenzie selected three white flannel flowers and two fronds of pink Geraldton wax, to provide some colour, tying them into a simple bunch with a piece of the silk the tailor had given her, probably intending it for her hair.

But she'd inherited her hair from her mother and in photos of her parents' wedding day, her mother had worn her hair swept up, and unadorned, even by a veil.

Now Kenzie smiled through threatening tears as she pictured those photos, realising that the dress she'd had the tailor make for her was almost a replica of her mother's—a simple sheath!

Muriel bounced into the room at that stage, so excited Kenzie suggested she sit a while to calm down. Dressed in an elegant, fitted dress, almost the exact pink of the Geraldton wax flowers Kenzie had chosen, Muriel looked beautiful, and Kenzie could see why so many men had loved her.

'Love's not enough,' Muriel said, as if Kenzie had spoken the words aloud. 'I've given it a lot of thought, this marriage of yours, and I'm beginning to think it's probably a far more sensible way to go. A kind of business arrangement with sex as a bonus. People talk about falling in love, but the problem is so many of them, me especially, fall out of it as well. So love isn't nearly as good a basis for marriage as something that's practical and sensible.'

The conversation then turned to the flowers, which the maid was arranging in vases all around the room.

'But they are beautiful!' Muriel exclaimed. 'Now, tell me all their names!'

'Not now,' Kenzie said firmly. 'I've got to do my hair and then we both need to head up to the penthouse suite. I won't be long.'

She went back into her bedroom, Muriel's voice following her, complaining that Kenzie hadn't taken her boss up on a promise to pay for the hairdresser, as Alex had paid for the gown instead.

* * *

Feeling decidedly foolish in the soft, cream shirt that hung out over his trousers, Alex paced the balcony. Gran was as good as he'd seen her since they'd arrived, and was arrayed in a spectacular scarlet bed jacket.

The priest had arrived and was sitting by the bed, talking quietly to her, while Robert was fussing around the room, arranging, on every horizontal surface, masses of the local orchids that grew wild on the island.

Horizontal—now there was a word.

Damn his brain!

For some reason, it was beavering away with thoughts—and even some rather risqué images—of his wedding night.

Not a thought for the ceremony itself.

And for all he was getting married to please Gran, the fact that he'd been attracted to his bride from the moment they'd met was causing all manner of doubts in his head.

And for a man of thirty-five to be suffering teenage angst—what if she's not physically attracted to me?—was ridiculous.

He heard the soft chime of the doorbell and

left his room to answer it, his breath catching in his throat as he saw the woman he was about to marry.

Her dark, dark hair swept up into a tumble of curls on the top of her head, a slim-fitting dress emphasising her curves, and little more than a dash of soft pink on her lips, and dark pencil enhancing her beautiful eyes, she was the loveliest thing he'd ever seen.

'Well,' Muriel said, bringing him back to earth with a thud. 'Are you going to ask us in?'

He held the door open, still wordless, and watched as she walked inside, going immediately to the bed set up in the huge lounge area where Gran was propped like a queen.

Now his wife-to-be was speaking softly to Gran, and he was still standing there holding the door.

'She does look beautiful, doesn't she?' Muriel said, linking her arm through his and drawing him away so she could close the door. 'And don't forget to tell her so—later, when you go to bed.'

Dear heaven, how was he going to get through this, especially now damn Muriel had put the 'bed' word back into his head. Okay, so it was five o'clock, the time when Gran was usually at her best, but even then there remained many hours to get through before—

He pulled himself together, and crossed the room, taking Kenzie's hand and telling her she looked beautiful. He would definitely tell her again later, but right now he needed to get with the programme.

The priest had left Gran's side, standing up, while Robert bustled about, positioning them behind a small table at the end of Gran's bed, the priest opposite them, Muriel by Kenzie's side, Robert himself finally taking his place beside the groom.

Him!

Kenzie's hand had turned so she clasped his as well, and somehow, with a pounding pulse and tingling nerves, words were said, promises exchanged, then Robert was popping the cork on an exorbitantly priced bottle of champagne, Kenzie was bent over Gran, explaining the flowers she was carrying were Australian natives, and Muriel had seated herself on one of the couches and was holding her champagne aloft in a toast to the newlyweds.

Not 'happy couple', Alex thought, and realised that he'd relaxed. All that stuff that had been going on in his head had been nothing more than nerves.

He took two fizzing glasses from Robert, and crossed to join Kenzie at Gran's side.

'Very sensible, my dear,' Gran was saying.

'And what has my wife—' he liked the sound of that '—been saying that's sensible?'

He handed one glass to Kenzie and raised his to toast her.

'Just that she's keeping her own name,' Gran replied. 'I suppose you were too carried away with the wedding to actually read the papers you were signing. I do wish your mother had kept Monroe—though she probably didn't think about it. People didn't, in those days.'

It took a moment for Alex to process this information. His brain *must* have been in a turmoil that he hadn't taken it in earlier.

But now he had processed it, he found he didn't like it.

'Because of your father?' he asked Kenzie. 'To keep the Steele name for this property you have?'

She grinned at him.

'No! There've been other names down through

the generations, but I could hardly get around introducing myself as McKenzie McLeod, now could I?'

She paused, then said, 'Do you mind? I didn't think it would matter, given the kind of marriage we're going into. I should have talked to you about it but, really, you wouldn't want to be married to someone called McKenzie McLeod, now, would you?'

Those darned blue eyes were laughing at him now, and it was all he could do not to sweep her into his arms, champagne flutes and all, and kiss those pale pink lips.

Would she respond enthusiastically?

Would those eyes cloud over with desire?

He closed his own eyes momentarily and breathed deeply.

Fortunately, Muriel saved him any embarrassment by announcing food had arrived, and Robert had magicked the little table where they'd signed their certificates into a place where they could sit and eat.

'Your gran's tiring,' Kenzie whispered to him as they moved to the table.

And he turned to see she'd closed her eyes,

and waved away the little silver table Robert was about to set up in front of her.

'I think we should go on down to my suite,' Muriel said quietly, and Robert nodded.

'I'll have the food sent down there,' he said.

'And I'll pop back to see Gran when we've eaten, in case she wakes again.'

Kenzie took his hand, and smiled at him.

'*We'll* come back and see her,' she said. 'I think she'd expect that.'

He gave the hand that held his a little squeeze, and accompanied the women out of the room.

Why this hand-holding thing was sending her heart into a flutter, Kenzie had no idea. This was a business arrangement, but the fluttering heart and the turmoil in her stomach seemed to think it was the real thing.

Well, it would be as far as—well, sex was concerned. They both wanted children so it was a given it would be part of the deal.

She followed Muriel and Alex out of the lift, and into Muriel's suite, pleased when Alex gave a gasp of astonishment at the array of flowers and insisted on learning what they all were.

And talking about the wildflowers eased her

tension, so the three of them sat down to eat from the array of dishes Robert had ordered for them.

Not that Kenzie really wanted food, her mind too occupied with what lay ahead. It was all very well, getting married in a hurry, getting married for purely business reasons, but they'd only exchanged one kiss.

One very hesitant kiss—so hesitant it hardly counted.

She glanced sideways at the man she'd so recently married, and wondered what it would be like to kiss him properly. He had lovely lips, if you could say that about a man's lips—nicely shaped and full but not too full, and—

'Out of here, the pair of you,' Muriel said, so suddenly Kenzie almost fell off her chair. 'You've got better things to be doing than sitting around with an old woman. And, Kenzie, dear, I know you were concerned about me when Robert organised for all your things to be taken up to Alex's rooms in the suite, but I'll be just fine. In fact, Gan is going to shift into your room and be my companion. I've fixed it all with the hotel.'

Kenzie's mouth opened, but no sound came

out, and she could only stare at her friend—well, employer really.

Then Alex was saying, 'That's grand! Thank you so much, Muriel, for all you've done for us both. We'll be off now.'

He caught Kenzie's hand in his, and all but dragged her to her feet before steering her inexorably towards the door.

Once in the lift, he pulled her closer to him, smiling down at her.

'That priest left out the "you may now kiss the bride" part of our wedding ceremony so I thought I'd do it now.'

Still trying to come to terms with Muriel and Gan, Kenzie could only stare at him, until his face was too close for focus, and his lips were on hers. It was a gentle hint of a kiss, but at the same time it was a promise.

More will come, it said.

More kisses and much, much more…

They had actually entered Alex's rooms—a small lounge room off his bedroom—before she realised they'd left the lift.

CHAPTER SEVEN

HE PUT HIS arms around her, and drew her to him, just holding her for a moment before kissing her again.

It was much more of a kiss than the earlier one, and it drew a response she couldn't remember ever feeling before. It heated blood not only in her silly cheeks but all through her body, so it seemed natural to press closer to his cool one.

And joined at the lips, they moved together, Kenzie unaware of the direction but, yes, it was into his bedroom.

Now his kiss became an exploration, his lips brushing the corners of her eyes, the small sensitive patch of skin beneath her ear, lips again, then trailing lower, always warm, but seeking, searching, learning her.

His ear was close, and she could kiss his jawline, slide her tongue along it, then up to touch his lips, bringing his lips back to give hers more attention.

Her lips parted to the gentle invasion of his tongue, then a few mumbled words—

Too many clothes?

Whatever!

Now he was sliding the zip down at the back of her dress, slipping it off her shoulders, while her own hands were clumsily undoing the buttons down his shirt.

Too slowly apparently, for he stripped it off over his head, baring his chest, a fuzz of dark hair across his breast.

She felt his skin against hers, as hot as hers, she rather thought, but thoughts were hard to come by as she lost herself in his pleasuring of her body.

'You are beautiful,' he said at some stage, the words muffled against her skin, tongue teasing at her nipples so she felt an ache between her thighs—an urgency for more.

All clothes gone now, he led her to the bed, but where she'd hoped for satisfaction, he was apparently far from finished with his exploration of her body.

Lips and fingers now, his mouth suckling

gently at one breast, and then the other, making her hold his head more tightly to her.

His hands slipped between them, fingers finding her sensitive nub. Teasing it now as his arousal pressed against her body.

How could she not take him, hold him, make him groan in return. He slid one finger into her and she tensed at the invasion, liking it, needing it, needing more.

But Alex was obviously not a man to be hurried as he continued to tease her while her hands roved his body, until they somehow rolled together, her on top of him, her hands sliding his erection into her moist, throbbing body.

A brush of his hands across her breasts, and she gasped and bit back a moan as her body climaxed and she collapsed on top of him, moving to tempt him further into her, teasing him in turn by pulling away, but never right away until he, too, gave a soft cry and dropped back, bearing them both onto their sides, bodies still joined, faces close, his expression one of surprise. An expression she was fairly certain was mirrored on *her* face.

'It was as if our bodies already knew each

other,' he said at last, and Kenzie snuggled closer, knowing exactly what he'd meant.

Had they slept that she woke, his back spooned around her? Desire hardening him again, exciting her, so she pushed against him until, still half–asleep, she thought, he entered her again, but not asleep for his arm was around her, his fingers stroking as he moved until, together, they reached orgasms that drew cries from both of them.

Surely then they slept, though Kenzie dreamed she'd lain close to him, her hands on his body, his on hers...

A roaring noise woke Kenzie, confusing her with its unfamiliarity, but then the bed was also unfamiliar, and memory returned.

Memories, plural, most of which brought her ever-ready blush not just to her cheeks but to her entire body.

She was glad of the semi-darkness as she remembered the excitement and surprising delight of the previous night. That she could have found—quite by accident, really—someone who was so well matched to her in bed was unbelievable.

Unbelievably wonderful, really.

And for a moment she lay and revelled in it, until the noise she'd heard became louder, more terrifying somehow.

She reached out a tentative arm, but the other side of the bed was empty.

Had Alex heard the noise and gone to investigate?

She listened, heard different noises—like screams and wails of anguish—distinctive, although she was on the top floor of the palace.

Instinct had her slipping out of bed, heading for the large balcony outside, when she realised she was naked.

Back inside, rummaging through the clothes in the suitcase she hadn't had time—it had been the kiss that had done it—to unpack the previous night.

She pulled on shorts and a baggy top and made her way outside, finding Alex there—naked—staring down at a scene of devastation below them.

But not even the sight of his naked body, lean and firm, or memories of what she'd shared with that body during the night could distract her from what lay below them.

Water swirled through the village, dragging everything in its wake as it receded towards the sea.

'What is it?' she asked 'What's happened.'

He put his arm around her.

'Tsunami, I imagine, though I've only heard of them, not seen one. This water is from the second wave I've seen come in. They seem to be getting smaller.'

'A tsunami—but that won't only be affecting this island, it will be swilling around villages on all the islands and on the mainland coast. How do such terrible things happen?'

'They're usually the result of an underwater earthquake but there should have been warnings—sirens and things.'

'We have to go down there—people will need help.'

He turned, pulled her into his arms and kissed her hard and fast.

'We'll get dressed first.' He was guiding her back into the bedroom, all practicality now.

'Wear something solid like trainers on your feet. We should grab something to eat. Robert's probably seeing to that right now.'

Back in their rooms, she stripped off the

clothes she'd pulled on. She definitely needed undies, and jeans. Jeans were tough. And that long-sleeved cotton shirt.

Ignoring the scent their lovemaking had left on her body—there was no time for a shower—she pulled on her clothes and met Alex in the small lounge room where he was already tucking into sandwiches while Robert packed a backpack with towels and a first-aid kit that looked large enough to belong in an ambulance.

'I've got a backpack,' she said as she grabbed a sandwich and hurried from the room as she bit into it. 'Bottled water, Robert,' she called back over her shoulder.

She emptied out her smaller backpack and carried it back to where Robert had produced a dozen bottles of water.

'We'll put the first-aid kit and a couple of bottles of water into yours and I'll take the rest of the water,' Alex said, and within minutes, still chomping on sandwiches, they left the room, having to run down the fire stairs as the lift wasn't working.

'This place has a generator so there'll be power before long,' Alex said, as they went down and down the twisting stairway. 'I wonder if the hospital was affected. It's further down the slope of the mountain.'

Kenzie closed her eyes momentarily and prayed things wouldn't be as bad as they had seemed from up high, but the lower they went, the clearer the anguished cries of torment and grief became.

Finally, on the ground floor, they found the manager already organising staff to clear the grand entrance foyer. He took one look at Alex and Kenzie and said, 'You can send people here. We have staff who can treat the injured or at least make them comfortable, and we can feed as many as we need to—water isn't a problem as we have our own spring.'

Alex nodded and turned to Kenzie.

'You should stay and help here,' he said.

'You think?' she replied, with a look that stopped further conversation.

They jogged down the drive, past the stables where the stablehands were trying to calm terrified animals—but at least it was dry, which meant any houses this high up would be okay.

But around the next bend they reached the high-water mark of the deadly tide that had devastated the tropical paradise. It must have swept in in the darkness then roared out again, taking houses, people and animals with it. All that was left was debris—a fallen palm here, the frond roof of a house there, broken bits of furniture, overturned cars and smashed tuk-tuks.

They'd both stopped, unable to believe the scene in front of them, then a cry from the left had them both turn that way.

A man was slumped against a still standing palm, crying out from pain and terror.

'Just be careful where you put your feet,' Alex said, in such a commanding voice Kenzie would probably have saluted had the situation not been so grim.

Stumbling through the chaos, they reached the man, who seized Alex's hand and babbled something totally incomprehensible.

Which obviously didn't bother Alex at all. He was crouched by the man, soothing him with words his listener wouldn't have understood either.

The man's right arm hung at an ugly angle from his shoulder. As Alex continued to examine the man, Kenzie reached into his backpack and drew out a bottle of water, holding it to the man's lips.

'I think it's just that shoulder,' Alex said as she bent close to him. 'Let's see if we can get him up, and we'll support him back to the stables and get one of the lads to take him up the palace. They'll have some form of pain relief in their pharmaceutical products.'

They eased the man to his feet.

'If you put his left arm around my shoulder I can take him,' Kenzie said. 'There'll be so many more that need help.'

Alex shook his head.

'You and I will stick together. We won't be the only able bodies out helping the injured, and we can do more together than separately.'

They'd reached the road and turned towards the stables when they heard the high-pitched crying of a child.

'You take him,' Kenzie said. 'I won't go far— just over there.'

She pointed to the ruin that had obviously been a house at one stage.

'I'll wait for you there, or come this way and meet up with you again,' she said to cut off his objection.

The cry was desperate, and she didn't wait for Alex to agree, simply headed off towards the noise, calling out that she was coming, although the likelihood of the child understanding her was slim.

She reached the wrecked building, seeing where the front wall had been sucked away by the receding wave. A tiny child, maybe one or two, sat on the ground in the middle of what once had been a room, screaming in terror at his abandonment in this devastated environment.

Still talking to him, soothingly and quietly now, she reached the child and knelt, smiling in spite of her concern. Felt all over his small body but could find no broken or dislocated bones.

She lifted him then, and held him close.

He'd been sitting near a grubby piece of material, possibly a sarong, and after rubbing him with a towel to dry and warm him, she fashioned a sling around her neck so she could carry him in front of her, his wails growing quieter as he was held close to her warm body.

Alex joined her and smiled at her inventiveness.

'He seems unhurt, just so dreadfully alone.'

Alex rubbed his hand over the child's head and drew a smile from the tiny boy.

'I'd offer to carry him but there may be debris to move and we don't want him harmed,' he said. 'And we'll stay up here near this tide mark as I think I'm right in saying they come as a series, these waves—the big one then maybe five or six to follow. I've seen two, so they should be getting much smaller.'

They'd treated five more people, most for minor wounds, before they found a woman curled up on the ground, a deep wound on her right thigh.

Alex knelt beside her, while Kenzie pulled out a water bottle and flushed the wound as best she could, then took some disinfectant from the first-aid kit and dabbed that around it.

'It needs stitching, but I'll wrap it tightly to stop further bleeding,' Alex said, but he looked worried.

Kenzie turned and saw what he'd seen—a long line of people making their way to the palace.

'You think we'd do more good up there?' she asked, and he nodded.

'I'm sure we would,' he said. 'Look down

below us, there are many people out searching, and if you see the number of people heading up the hill, even if they aren't all injured, we should be there, helping.'

He reached out and wiped some dirt off her sleeve—smiled—and her body shivered with the memories of the intense passion they'd shared.

'But first we need to get this woman up there. I've checked her out and her left ankle's very swollen—she won't even be able to limp along.'

He hesitated, looking around before turning to Kenzie.

'She's small. Do you think you're up to helping carry her, if we cross our arms and she sits between us? We need only get as far as the road, where someone else will surely help.'

'We have to get her to her feet first,' Kenzie pointed out.

Together they bent over the woman once more, Alex explaining what they needed to do, although it was doubtful she understood. But once they had her on her feet, Alex supporting her against his body, she seemed to understand what they were doing, and not only sat on their joined hands but put her arms around their necks to keep herself balanced there.

Alex had already taken Kenzie's backpack and had it slung over his free shoulder, so they turned towards the road and made their way unsteadily through the debris towards it.

'You okay?' he asked. 'We could put her down while you go ahead to get help.'

She grinned at him.

'I'm fine. We breed 'em tough in northern Australia!'

He flashed a smile in her direction then nodded to the now sleeping child.

'Breed 'em tough here, too, the way he's sleeping with your arm squashed against him.

'I'm trying *not* to squash him,' she retorted, 'although I realise now I should have moved him to my back before we set out. But if I stop now, we'll never make it.'

They plodded on, and were almost at the road when they were spotted, two apparently uninjured men coming towards them.

'We will take her,' one said, and Kenzie smiled at him, pleased he could speak English but even more pleased to be relieved of one of her burdens.

Alex organised the transfer, then took Kenzie's hand and they all walked together up the hill...

Chaos reigned at the Palace of Peace and Contentment.

Alex took one look, and told Kenzie to go and get cleaned up, then found the manager, who was staring around at his beautiful foyer with a look of dazed incredulity.

'Most of these people aren't hurt but all of them could be carrying any manner of germs, so could you stand up somewhere and tell all those who are not injured to go over to the swimming pool and shower in the cabana there?' He told the man. 'They can wash their clothes and put them back on, then stay outside in the sun, unless they have an injured child and need to return to him or her.'

The man nodded.

'I'll send some staff to keep them in order while they wait,' he said. 'We *have* tried to keep the badly injured away from the less injured, but it's hard with so many people.'

'You just get the uninjured out, and have staff down by the stables to stop more uninjured coming. I know they'll want to look for loved ones, but right now we need to help those who need help.'

He left the manager climbing a few steps to get above the crowd and went to where people lay on a line of beds.

They must have pulled every unused bed from the suites above him. The man with the injured shoulder was sitting on the end of one of them, talking quietly to a woman who lay on it.

Someone—one of the nursing staff presumably—had fashioned a sling for him, and given him pain relief for him to be speaking so clearly in what was probably his second language.

He'd make a handy interpreter, Alex decided, and asked his name.

'Lamon,' the man replied, smiling brightly.

He'd definitely been given pain medication.

'Have you spoken to this woman?' Alex asked.

'It is her back, she cannot move her toes,' Lamon said.

'The hospital?' Alex asked, and the man shook his head.

'Water all through it, though the building is

still standing. But the helicopter, it is all right, up there on the top,' Lamon told him.

Which meant that they could get the badly injured to hospital on the mainland if they could find the pilot.

He'd moved to the next bed, where a man lay on his side in the recovery position, while an older woman, he presumed a nurse, was washing mud from his body.

'It's hard to tell if they're hurt, with all the mud,' she said, then her eyes filled with tears.

'My family, down in the village, all the people are saying the village is gone.'

Alex patted her shoulder, checked the man's pulse and wondered where, in the Palace of Peace and Contentment, he'd find a stethoscope, thermometer, and boxes of gloves.

At least!

'Here we are,' a bright voice said behind him, and, while his body thrilled to the voice, he turned to find Kenzie, not only clean, and with the small child now strapped to her back, but pushing a trolley with a goodly array of medical equipment on it.

'Do we need the baby? Could you not find anyone to take him?'

'I didn't try,' his new bride said. 'He knows me now, and what's more, if he's there on my back someone might recognise him and claim him.'

Alex nodded. She was obviously thinking more clearly than he was.

'Antiseptic will be the big problem,' she told him now. 'Their storeroom doesn't seem to keep it in gallon containers like we do at the hospital.'

He grinned at her, ignoring the very surprising memories of the night before—that they'd been so physically well suited was nothing short of a miracle—and reached out for a stethoscope.

'This is Lamon,' he said, gesturing towards his helper. 'And I've a horrible feeling that this man on the bed has inhaled some of the mud he must have been buried in.'

He'd adjusted the stethoscope and was leaning over to listen to the man's chest as he spoke.

'That's two who should be in hospital,' he said as he straightened.

They found the woman with the cut thigh in the next bed. Lamon talked quietly to the woman in her own language while Kenzie undid their rough bandage and he, Alex, checked her chest.

It sounded clear, but the wound Kenzie had now revealed was far uglier than he'd thought in the dim light of early dawn.

'Is there much local anaesthetic?' he asked, and Kenzie shook her head.

'Ten ampoules,' she told him, 'and I'd say that wound needs a couple.'

'We treat her!' he said, in a no-nonsense voice. 'Holding onto some and finding it's not needed would be worse than not having some for someone further down the line. Other help will come. Emergency response teams will be gathering all around the world and by tomorrow the first will arrive.'

Obscurely comforted by his optimistic words, she pulled on clean gloves and picked up some tweezers, broke them out of their sealed bag, then leaned in to tweeze tiny pieces of grit from the wound.

Alex watched as he changed his gloves and found an ampoule of local anaesthetic, drawing it up into a syringe.

'Try squirting the debris out with a syringe filled with water,' he suggested. 'Leave it a few minutes for the anaesthetic to work. I'll give her two.'

And though he was concentrating on his patient, he was also aware of Kenzie by his side as she tidied the dirty bandages into the bin on the bottom shelf of the trolley, adjusted the precious bundle on her back, and filled a syringe with water.

Weird how just looking at her brought warmth to his body even in this emergency situation.

Ignoring thoughts he shouldn't be thinking, Alex sorted through the things Kenzie had scavenged for the trolley, finding plenty of sutures.

Were the usual guests at the palace so clumsy that sutures were often needed, or had they been ordered in bulk and not used?

'I think that's clean, I'll check ahead,' Kenzie said. 'There are two French nurses on staff here and they're working from the other end, but now someone's cleared away all the onlookers, it's much easier to see what's what.'

Practical woman! Alex thought with a sense of gratitude that by pure luck he'd found her.

Concentrate on the job!

He bent low over the patient, setting the sutures carefully into place, leaving the ends to trim off later. She'd need antibiotics—would the palace have a supply of them as well?

'Alex!'

Kenzie called to him from two beds down.

'Two minutes,' he told her and finished his job, smearing antibacterial cream over the wound before covering it with a padded dressing and bandaging it again.

The man two beds down was another who definitely should be in hospital, with his broken tibia poking through his skin.

'There's a note saying he's been given morphine for the pain, but we can't fix this, can we?' Kenzie said.

Alex knelt to study the wound, shaking his head at the severity of the break.

'There's some bleeding but no major vessel involvement. We can fashion a splint,' he told her. 'Did you see anything that looked like splint material when you raided the supply cupboard?'

Kenzie shook her head, frowned, then said, 'No, but when I was searching for the supply cupboard I noticed some wooden packing cases out the back of the building. I'm sure we could rip the slats off them to use. Pad them with something soft and they'll be fine. I'll go and get some. Three?'

But before he could speak, she was gone.

Time to move on—he'd return to the man when Kenzie came back, though he couldn't imagine what would come in wooden packing cases.

He was too busy to wonder what was taking her so long until she returned, holding up three padded and bandage-wrapped pieces of wood that he knew he could fashion into an open splint to protect the leg when the patient was transported.

When? That was the question, and, he supposed, how? He doubted boats would put to sea while the waves from the tsunami were still making the waters dangerous.

With Kenzie's help and a little ingenuity, he then splinted the man's leg and bandaged it to protect the open wound and jagged edge of the bone.

'Time for a break, you two,' a voice said, and there was Muriel, with a middle-aged man, presumably Gan, smiling beside her. He was pushing a trolley with an urn on it, paper cups, milk and sugar, teabags and little sachets of coffee.

On the lower shelf were piles of sandwiches.

'It was all I could think of to do that might help,' Muriel said, in rather apologetic tones. 'The kitchen staff are all too busy making soup and rice for all the people outside. And, of course, meals for the guests, most of whom really want to leave,' she added. 'So Gan and I did this.'

But Alex, suddenly realising he was famished, practically hugged her.

'Now stop,' she said, in her usual commanding way, 'and have a proper break while you drink and eat. Just tell me what you want to drink and I'll fix it, then help yourself to sandwiches and go sit on the steps and eat them.'

Alex glanced over to the grand, sweeping stairway that was a feature of the palace's foyer and was relieved to see half a dozen people sitting there, all eating and drinking, no one talking much, except in occasional murmurs.

CHAPTER EIGHT

NIGHT HAD FALLEN before they had all the patients still on the premises as comfortable as they could make them. But more were still dribbling in and Alex was trying to persuade Kenzie to go up to the room and have a rest.

One of the local staff had recognised the baby, and was happy to care for him, no doubt because she, like so many others here, had lost family in the village.

They joined the manager on the stairs, and saw the pain on the man's face.

'So many of our household staff and nurses lived in the village. A few have been found and come to us here, but I fear the loss will be great.'

It was such a sobering thought there was silence for a moment.

'Can you carry on?' Alex eventually asked.

The manager nodded.

'We have enough live-in nurses to cover the

guests here at the moment, if they accept extra shifts, which they all will. But after this, without the village, will people even want to come?'

Seeing a large man, his right arm swathed in bandages up to his shoulder, coming through the door, Kenzie left Alex talking to the manager and headed for the new victim.

He was tall, and solidly built, and liberally sprinkled with mud. What she could see of the skin on his face was grey with pain and fatigue.

But before she could reach him, he planted both feet on the floor and in a voice that could probably have been heard on the mainland, called out, 'I don't suppose any of you can fly a chopper.'

'I can,' Kenzie responded, walking quickly towards him. 'We use them for mustering back home.'

'Good,' he said. 'The chopper's fine, I just can't fly it, but word is you have some people with bad injuries. We can take two on stretchers, and two seated. One of my boys is bringing the stretchers now.'

Bemused by the conversation—it had been a very long day—Kenzie said, 'You want me to fly your chopper. I'd have no idea where to go.'

'I'll be with you, mate,' he said, the last word convincing her that he was, as she'd thought from his accent, another Aussie.

'Are you mad?'

Alex was standing beside her, one hand on her shoulder. 'You're going to fly this man's helicopter?'

'Well, he can't,' Kenzie said, pointing at the man. 'He's barely made it here. If I get him over to a mainland hospital, there's sure to be another pilot who can fly it back with me, *and* whatever medical supplies I can scrounge because you know as well as I do there are still more people coming in.'

'Ah, here's my boy. Where are your patients?' the stranger said.

Kenzie turned to see a young Thai man holding two collapsible stretchers.

'Maybe the man with the leg wound can sit,' she said, turning to Alex who was looking slightly dazed.

'You can't go flying off in some strange helicopter,' he said, then smiled ruefully. 'That was a stupid thing to say, wasn't it? You wouldn't have offered if you couldn't do it. I really don't know why I'm surprised.'

And still shaking his head, he took the stretchers from the young man and carried them over to their two unconscious patients.

The French nurses who'd been enjoying a break on the stairs immediately went to help him, while Kenzie led the stranger—stranger? Angel of mercy, more like—over to the man with the badly broken leg.

'I'm Kenzie,' she said as they made their way across the foyer, 'and the man you were talking to is Alex, a Scottish doctor.

'Brad,' the man said, holding out his left hand. 'Nice to meet another Aussie.'

But that was going to be the limit of any conversation for the man was clearly exhausted and, of course, Muriel had appeared from nowhere with Gan and the food and drink trolley.

While she hurried Brad over to the stairs, and Alex and the two nurses were getting the wounded onto stretchers, she reached the man with the broken leg and was glad to find Lamon, who'd acted as interpreter for them all day, sitting on the floor by the man's bed.

'We want to take him over to the hospital on

the mainland in the helicopter,' she told Lamon, 'but he will have to sit up. We'll make him as comfortable as possible. Could you ask him if he thinks he can manage that?'

Lamon spoke to the very drowsy patient, who nodded and proceeded to sit up on the bed.

'No, just wait,' Kenzie said, holding up her hand. 'We need to work out how we're going to get you to the helicopter.'

'I'll find you help,' Lamon said, and disappeared out the door, returning only minutes later with five men, mostly young and all fit-looking.

'Some of my soccer team,' Lamon said proudly, and Kenzie nodded at them all.

'They were by the pool, safe, not like so many others, even my family,' Lamon said, and Kenzie could only wonder at how the survivors were going to cope when the shock of the tsunami was over and reality set in.

'Here's a chair.' Alex had appeared by her side, holding both a chair and a sheet. 'I feel I should come, but the woman with the head wound will need the other seat.'

The concern on his face was evident, and the

fact that he wanted to travel with them all—and her especially?—warmed her heart.

'And you're far more useful here,' she said. 'Because wounded people are still being found and brought in.'

He nodded, but looked far from happy.

Because she could fly a helicopter and he couldn't?

Probably not, she told herself. Perhaps he cared?

She dismissed that thought as well, and listened to his explanation.

'If we tie our man with the broken leg into it, he can be carried to the chopper. The splint at the back of his leg comes up above his knee so it can't be bent. I'll take one side so I can be sure the injured leg doesn't crash into anything.'

Kenzie could only watch as he and Lamon set up the makeshift ambulance and settled the man on it. Soccer players were already lifting the stretchers, and Brad, revived no doubt by food and coffee, was giving orders about the best way to get along the side of the hill.

'There's a better track above the high-water

mark,' Lamon said. 'All the boys know it. Just follow them.

'We don't know what's under the top layer of mud,' Lamon said to Alex, 'so it's best to stay on the track.'

Brad was plodding valiantly along, while Kenzie had Adele, one of the French nurses, help her with the woman with the heavily bandaged head.

They were soon plunged into darkness as they entered the thick jungle, and now only torches supplied by the hotel lit the way.

It seemed to take for ever—first to reach the helicopter, and then to get everyone settled and strapped in.

Alex helped Kenzie into the pilot's seat, held her hand for a moment, his eyes on hers, unreadable.

Finally, he gave her hand a squeeze, and said, 'Come back safe.' And something in those softly spoken words brought tears to her eyes.

Brad climbed into the seat next to her.

'I've done a ground inspection,' he said, as she began checking the controls. It was an unfamiliar aircraft, but having flown many different choppers she knew the set-up would be similar and easy to handle.

'It's only a twenty-minute flight to the city,' Brad said, 'but the chopper might not make it back tonight. The other side will be as bad as this and a spare pilot might be hard to find.'

He was speaking across her to Alex, who merely nodded, touched Kenzie's hand again and shut her door.

'I don't have a commercial licence,' Kenzie said, as she started the engine.

Brad smiled tiredly at her.

'Do you think those folk we've got back there will care?'

He strapped himself in, handed headphones to Kenzie and put his own on.

'Just take her up and head east,' he said. 'I'll alert the authorities we're airborne and give you directions. No good trying the hospital we usually use on the coast. That will be in chaos. We'll go to the regional hospital in town. We can land on the roof there.'

He was leaning back, his eyes closed as he spoke, and as Kenzie lifted them into the air and headed east, she hoped like hell he didn't pass out completely or she'd be flying around looking for a building with a big helicopter cross on a pad on its roof.

She could fly a *helicopter*?

Alex had headed back along the track, his eyes on the noisy aircraft until he plunged into the darkness of the forest and the sound of it slowly died away.

He wondered why he was surprised. This was a woman who'd agreed to marry him when she barely knew him, why wouldn't she have a helicopter licence?

Yet a knotted feeling deep in his gut, suggested he wasn't quite as relaxed about this as he'd have liked to be.

He arrived back at the hotel, and after checking on the other wounded went upstairs to shower and see his grandmother.

'She's been in a deep sleep all day,' Robert told him. 'Which is probably just as well. It would not be good for her to see what has happened.'

'You're right,' Alex replied, feeling heavy hearted himself over the destruction. 'I'll have a shower and come and sit with her.'

'You should sleep,' Robert said sternly, and Alex found a tired smile.

'I can sleep in the chair after I've read a little more of the story.'

He went through to his own rooms to peel off his dirty clothes and shower. And as he walked through the bedroom, how could he not help but look at the bed, pristinely made, yet all he saw was Kenzie, naked in the rumpled sheets.

He shook his head, thinking again of their night of lovemaking—thinking how unlikely it had been—two people who barely knew each other being so well matched in passion.

But the thought that followed was less pleasing—an image of Kenzie at the controls of the helicopter, imagining her flying over the devastation on both sides of the gulf—

With the shower on full blast, he washed away further thoughts of accidents, and of the devastation they'd both seen. She'd be over land again by now, and he was thankful for the darkness, as if it might prevent her seeing how bad things were on the mainland shore.

He knew from memories of the last huge tsunami in the Indian Ocean that over one hundred thousand people had lost their lives. And as he rubbed himself dry, he sent a silent prayer to any god who might be listening that the death toll from this one would not be as horrendous.

Kenzie, exhausted but pleased Brad had found someone to fly back to the island, made her way along the track. The new pilot had elected to stay with the aircraft, explaining he could be called back for some rescue work.

The young Thai who was Brad's offsider met them, and said he'd organise to get the medical supplies she'd picked up down to the palace in the morning.

So she walked alone, concentrating on putting one foot in front of the other, so she could make it back.

A shower, then sleep—sleep for ever, the way she felt.

Was Alex at least resting?

Would his ER conscience let him go up to his rooms and sleep, or keep him on the ground floor with the patients?

He wasn't there, she discovered, coming in to find nurses she hadn't seen before cleaning and bandaging wounds, Housekeeping staff cleaning the floors—a full-time job, it seemed.

'We're night staff usually,' one of nurses told her, 'but others are doing our shift and some of our guests have said to help here rather than stay with them. The doctor has his pager. We call him if he's needed.'

Pleased that at least in this corner of the island things were peaceful at the moment, Kenzie made her way up to the penthouse, grateful the lift was now working. No way would she have made it up the fire-escape stairs.

No Alex in the room. The surge of disappointment surprised her as she'd believed she was too exhausted to feel any kind of unnecessary emotion.

But once she'd showered and pulled on her familiar old T-shirt that had been serving her as nightwear, she found she didn't want to get into the bed on her own.

She crept through the small sitting area, quietly opening the door into the larger room where his grandmother lay.

He was reading to her, something she didn't recognise, but the sound of his voice was so soothing she crept a little further in and lay down on the sofa, pulling a cushion beneath her head and falling asleep immediately.

* * *

Too exhausted to read for a moment longer, Alex closed the book and put it on the small side-table. He took his grandmother's hand, and held it as he eased the chair back into a comfortable position and closed his eyes.

He was on the edge of sleep when a muffled sound, more a small snort than a snore, had him sitting bolt upright. Thinking it must have been one of Gran's nurses, he looked around but there was no one moving in the room.

Another small sound, barely there, and he stood up.

Kenzie was on the sofa, sound asleep, her hands tucked under her head, a T-shirt with an animal of some kind on it covering her slim and beautiful body.

He looked around the darkened room, subtly lit by a few low-set nightlights, and found a soft angora throw he'd bought for Gran many years ago.

Carefully, he tucked it around his sleeping wife—he liked the word—liked even thinking it in his head.

Probably the novelty of it?

He smiled to himself, suspecting it could be more than that...

No, more likely exhaustion creating fancies in his head...

Back in his chair, he closed his eyes, content to be where he was—and somehow pleased that Kenzie was so close to him.

Was it the movement of Gran's hand in his that woke him?

Whatever! He was awake, and in the slow dawning of the new day he could see she was, too.

Her fingers stroked the back of his hand, fleetingly, a touch barely there, her lips parted, and she breathed his name. 'Alexander Monroe...'

No, not his name at all but her husband's!

She smiled, her eyes closed, and as her breathing changed, he leant in and kissed her cheek.

'I love you, Gran,' he whispered, and as his stomach knotted and his heart clenched with sadness, he knew it was goodbye.

CHAPTER NINE

KENZIE WOKE NOT to wails of terror this time but the clatter-clacking noise of a helicopter.

She looked around, her head woolly with sleep, certain she hadn't gone to bed in Alex's bed when she had got back from the mainland.

And the chopper she could hear wasn't the one she'd flown last night.

Was Alex right? Was aid beginning to come in to the devastated village?

Alex?

Where was he?

His side of the bed certainly hadn't been slept in.

She eased out of bed, smiling when she saw her night attire—habit had taken her back to her comfy old T-shirt...

All but sleepwalking, she made her way into the shower, hoping a good drenching would wake her up, because there were sure to be things she could still be doing to help the stricken island.

She found herself wanting—almost needing—to see Alex. To be near him, not even talking to him, just, yes, needing to see him.

A workaholic from all accounts, he'd be downstairs where survivors would still be coming in. The aid coming in would organise large-scale rescues, all to plan, and set up temporary shelters, arrange food and water, but until they could complete their preparations people would still come here.

And she should be there, helping.

She dressed in knee-length shorts and a sensible shirt, and slipped her feet into trainers, realising as she did up the laces that she was hungry.

Very hungry!

Hopefully, Muriel and Gan would still be manning their food trolley.

As she opened the door leading out to the penthouse foyer, she was greeted by Robert.

'I have been listening for you to wake up,' he said, and she smelled coffee and Danish pastries, and could have hugged the man.

She followed him as he carried it into the small sitting room.

'Mrs Monroe?' she asked, and Robert shook his head.

'Still alive, but barely. Alex spent the night by her bed, and now has gone downstairs to help where he can. He has a pager, you know, and I can get him back here any time.'

Kenzie nodded, and sat down beside the tray, wondering why she'd never given a minute's thought to what would happen when Alex's grandmother did die.

Because too much had happened too soon?

Because she'd seen this marriage as an answer to her immediate desires and not thought much beyond that.

So think now.

Presumably he'd want to fly her body back to her beloved Scotland.

And he would accompany it, for there'd certainly be nothing to keep him here.

Drink your coffee and eat a pastry, she told herself, aware that she was still tired enough to get weepy over trifles.

Not that Gran's death would be a trifle.

It would be a blessed release both for her and for Alex, but that wouldn't stop Alex feeling a heavy load of grief.

Should she go with him?

Would he want her to?

Would he accept whatever concern and support she could offer?

Useless thinking! Eat your pastry, drink your coffee, and get downstairs to find something useful to do.

Alex's heart stopped for an instant, as his wife, lovely hair neatly plaited back behind her head, came into the foyer.

She's beautiful, was his first thought, then his heart stuttered momentarily, but before she could tell him Gran had died—the thought that had caused the stutter—she smiled at him and he knew all was well.

Although 'well' was hardly the current state of affairs in his life, what with his grandmother, the complete devastation of this beautiful island, and the grief and hopelessness of its gentle people.

But still smiling she came towards him.

'Robert says you're to go up and have what he calls a proper breakfast, including black pudding no doubt.' She grimaced as if she'd once tried that particular treat and hadn't been impressed. 'But I told him you probably wouldn't. Have you had any more serious casualties while I was skiving off—sound asleep in bed?'

'Two have gone up to the hospital helicopter, and will be going straight into hospital, but most of the others are patch up their wounds and wait. The pilot who flew you back came down this morning with the medical supplies you brought with you, and that's been a great help.'

He paused, unsure whether to tell her more.

Leave her smiling?

She had such an open, happy smile...

'But?' she said. 'And don't deny there is a but, I could hear it in your voice.'

He smiled and touched her lightly on the shoulder.

Wanting to touch her.

Needing to touch her?

'The pilot is reluctant to take any but the

most serious of cases to the hospital as it's already been overrun from people affected on the mainland coast.'

He paused, thinking about what he'd experienced in emergency situations like these.

'He's right!' he added. 'Over here the rescue teams will have a field hospital set up in no time, including, even here on the island, a small but efficient operating theatre.'

'I'd read about that kind of response,' she said, frowning slightly as she considered the information. 'Fully staffed?'

'Not the first response team because they bring with them everything *they* need for a few days from food and water, to accommodation, showers, etcetera, and mostly first-aid equipment. They can assess the situation and advise what else is needed and when. Sanitation is usually the most important practical issue, then food and accommodation, although that will be further down the list here where it's not raining or snowing.'

'You've done this before?" she asked, surprise evident in both the question and her face.

'Earthquake in northern Italy,' he said briefly,

'and once in northern Greece after a massive forest fire.'

She shook her head.

'No wonder you've found being here so frustrating. It makes what you're doing for your grandmother even more impressive.'

'Even more?' he echoed, a smile tugging at his lips. 'You've been impressed?'

'Very,' she said firmly. 'Now, stop fishing for compliments and tell me what I can do. Who needs a nurse right now?'

I do was hardly an appropriate answer, so he took her along the line of beds, explaining each injury, pointing out those with fluid bags nearly empty, and other patients who needed new dressings on their wounds.

He'd reached the final patient, the woman whose leg they'd stitched—kept in because of the unsanitary conditions outside and needing to keep an eye on her wound.

'How's she doing?' Alex asked the nurse, but her reply was interrupted by his pager going off in his pocket.

'I'm sorry, I have to go, it's Gran, but I wanted to check the patients first.'

He was looking so worried Kenzie touched his arm and looked into his eyes.

'Go,' she said. 'She's the one who matters now—she and you!'

But as he left, she wondered what lay ahead.

Within minutes, the manager had appeared at the reception desk—kept in a clear, red-roped off space on the far side of the foyer.

Another man, the assistant manager, she thought, soon joined them, and some weighty discussion was obviously going on.

Then a maid appeared at Kenzie's shoulder.

'Mr Robert in the penthouse called. He asks for you to come.'

Gran's dead.

That was all it could be.

Had Alex been in time to say goodbye.

These thoughts chased her to the lift and, as she rose to the top floor, they kept at bay all the uncertainty of what lay immediately ahead.

A pale but dry-eyed Alex met her at the door.

'Your gran has died?'

He nodded, and she hesitated, but for only an instant, before wrapping her arms around him and holding him against her.

Was it the wrong thing to do?

For all they were married and had definitely enjoyed their wedding night, they barely knew each other as people, but instinct told her bereaved people needed physical comfort.

Even Alex?

She was thinking of pulling back when he moved, his arms going around her, holding her close, his cheek resting against her head.

He eased her into the room and closed the door, still holding tightly to her.

'I'll have to take her home to Scotland,' he said, 'to be buried near the husband she so loved. There's been a plane on standby over on the mainland for weeks now. It's been free to do other local flights but always aware this was coming up.'

Barely understanding the logistics of this, she nodded, then leaned away enough to tip her head so she could see his face.

'Would you like me to come with you? It would be a long way home with only your memories for company.'

A slight smile tilted one corner of his lips.

'That would be a very wifely thing to do.'

It was a half-tease, and the tension in her body eased. He would have come to terms with his grandmother's death some time ago, so maybe his grief now would be easier to handle.

'I *am* your wife!' she reminded him, then paused before adding, 'But no black pudding!' so she could see a proper smile.

He released her, stepping back and running his hand through his hair—looking more distracted than she'd ever seen him.

'There's so much to think about, even though I made all the plans, step by step, before we came out here, but now...'

'Now you can't think about them, so do whatever needs to be done first—the plane presumably—and we'll think about the rest later.'

'You *will* come?'

He sounded so hopeful she felt a flutter of excitement, not exactly in her heart but definitely in the region of her chest.

'Of course,' she said, and he smiled and pulled her close again.

'Thank you,' he said. 'I'm back on track now.'

She eased away from him.

'That sounds more like the man I know. Can I help?'

He looked at her for a moment.

'Pack?' he said, and smiled. 'Though I imagine your island clothes won't be quite sufficient for our Edinburgh winter.'

'I'll get something when I get there,' she said. 'I'm sure they have shops in Edinburgh.'

'If you don't mind wearing my clothes until you get to the shops,' he said.

He bent and kissed her lightly on the lips.

'I must rush,' he said. 'We've got a helicopter coming for us at four. It'll land on the hospital pad in the city. Can you be ready by then?'

'Of course,' she said, and went over to the door that led to their two rooms.

Of course, she didn't have anything suitable for an Edinburgh winter, but there were online shops all over the world. If she got busy now, they could have some clothes waiting for her by the time she arrived.

She'd need an address—but Robert would have that. Save her bothering Alex.

Robert would know what she should buy—and where!

She had a feeling the where was important for the people who inhabited Alex's world.

* * *

Robert not only told her where but produced a list of what she'd need, assuring her she could find everything she'd need from a couple of online stores.

He advised some warm layers for under her clothes. Next came skirts and warm sweaters, coats, both weatherproof and woollen. Tweed was always good, and cashmere very nice.

Kenzie's mind boggled at the list but they were leaving at four and she needed to get on-line. She figured if she had enough clothes to last a couple of days, she'd find time to visit the shops herself.

It was a hurried choice, and given the circumstances, and having known Gran slightly, she went for mostly formal blacks and greys in choosing outer clothing, though she found an irresistible dark blue coat with a mock fur collar and a tight-fitting hat to match and added them to her purchases.

The total made her gasp, but she had to phone her father to tell him what was happening, and he'd soon transfer more money to her credit card.

Money! What should she do about that? She'd need some cash to carry around.

In what?

The backpack she'd been using here?

Back onto the online store, she went to handbags, chose one and added it to the list, though what she'd ever do with a cashmere coat and leather handbag back in Darwin, where she mainly shopped, she didn't know!

Though she did know the leather handbag was likely to go mouldy the first wet season…

Alex packed while Robert handled his grandmother's things. He knew the plane had cabin connectivity so he could make any necessary phone calls on the journey.

And he was thinking about this because?

Because he wanted to be busy, thinking of other things, not wanting to inspect the knotting of his gut that had happened when Kenzie had said she'd come.

He should have hugged, her, told her that was wonderful. After all, she'd hugged him when she'd heard the news.

But nothing in his upbringing had taught him how to express his feelings—his relief…

His delight?

He thought about the word and realised that's exactly what it was. Delight that she wanted to be with him at this time, delight that someone cared enough.

Really, just delight about the woman he'd married so precipitously!

He should have hugged her...

Monroes don't do emotion!

The flight to Scotland was uneventful. Kenzie had worn jeans and the only long-sleeved top she'd brought with her, with her now battered trainers on her feet.

Checking her across the aisle, sleeping soundly, Alex was again glad she'd wanted to come. She'd divert attention from him while he went through all the business that had to be done—the funeral, and all that entailed in organisation, the reading of the will, and seeing its provisions were set in motion, decisions about Gran's flat in Edinburgh, then her country estate, and a check that all was well there.

And much as he longed to get back to work, to lose himself once more in something that provided interest, and escape from emotion, he knew there was much to do before he could turn away from his duties.

Having Kenzie there would alleviate some of the aggravation all this would cause...

Poor thing, he thought as he looked across at her, she had no idea what lay ahead of her.

CHAPTER TEN

'I DON'T KNOW why I was concerned about how you'd manage in such an alien environment,' Alex said to Kenzie when, within minutes of their arrival at his flat, she'd had a shower and washed her hair, reappearing in a pair of warm navy slacks and a soft blue jumper, her wet hair pulled back from her face by a band he thought might be what's called an Alice band.

'And as those are certainly not my clothes you're wearing, how did you manage that trans-formation.'

She grinned at him, thinking of the journey from the airport with her wrapped in his warm camel coat.

'Internet shopping, and a list from Robert of what I might need to begin with.'

He shook his head and smiled at her.

'Ahead of me at every turn,' he said. 'But I can tell from the cut and quality of those clothes they'll have cost plenty. Just how did you pay? I should have been giving you money, shouldn't I?

Her turn to smile.

'I have plenty of my own, thank you,' she informed him. 'Let me worry about my personal finances. Get on and do what you have to do so you can get back to work, which is really what you want to do. Right now, we should eat and go to bed, so we're both fresh in the morning. Robert says he's ordered dinner for us both to be sent in, though where from I've no idea.'

At that moment, the front doorbell chimed, so she assumed she was about to find out where dinner appeared from, and what it might contain.

'Someone knows how to cook good beef,' she said between mouthfuls some time later. 'This is delicious.'

'Knowing Robert, he's ordered it from the best restaurant in Edinburgh. My grandmother always ate there until she became ill, and that's when he started having small amounts of food sent in for her.'

Kenzie studied him for a moment, looking vaguely puzzled.

'He's going to miss her as much as you do,' she said quietly. 'Has he somewhere he can go?'

Alex stopped eating, knife and fork both poised in mid-air.

'Damn, I hadn't thought of Robert, although now I *do* think about it, he has a small landholding up near Gran's home in Wester-Ross— that's in the northern Highlands. He might go back there, or he— I just don't know.'

'If he wants to keep working, could he work for you?'

Alex sighed.

'If he does want to keep working, he'd certainly be welcome. I know he must have organised cleaners to come into this flat so it would be clean and tidy when we returned. Although would you care to have him around?'

Kenzie had to smile.

'Are you asking if I'd prefer to do not only my own washing and ironing and cleaning and tidying, and yours too, for that matter, then no! I'm not made for doing nothing—well, nothing but housework—I'd want to work as well.'

'Surgical nursing, right?'

She nodded.

'I might be able arrange something. I certainly can talk to a few people, and find out exactly what's involved.'

They finished their meal with amiable chit-chat, eating slowly, or so Kenzie felt.

She was exhausted after the rush to leave the island and long flight, but felt lost about the protocol of going to bed with her business partner in this marriage, without the wedding excitement, and their tentative kisses that had led them inexorably into bed the first night.

Did she just get in and wait?

But what side? He'd have a particular side for sure, but both bedside tables were clear, apart from a small lamp on each. Whoever Robert had sent in had done the job thoroughly.

The wardrobes had been easier, one full of obviously male clothes, so she'd arranged her meagre belongings in the other one.

And what to wear to bed was another problem. That first night—and her colour rose thinking about it—clothes had not been needed, and though the rooms here were warm, centrally heated, she felt embarrassed about getting into one of the silky little numbers she'd bought on the island.

She took off her elegant new clothes, and in bra and panties—far too pretty to be called plain old undies—she went into the bathroom to have a wash and clean her teeth.

Should she have another shower?

But she'd had one earlier and as Alex had been on the phone since they'd hit the ground, he might be ready for one now...

Who'd have thought married life could be so difficult?

Back in the bedroom, she was standing at the bottom of the bed, struggling with these problems, when Alex walked in.

'Very fetching!' he said with a smile in his voice. 'I'll just have a quick shower and join you in bed.'

And with that, he disappeared into the bathroom.

Leaving Kenzie exactly where she'd been before his appearance with the dilemma of which side of the bed.

Damn it all, she wasn't dumb.

She marched to the door and pushed it open, taking a minute to enjoy the lean, flat-muscled length of his body.

'Which side do you sleep on?' she asked, above the splash of the water.

He opened the glass door and smiled at her.

'Whichever side you're on,' he said, then laughed as heat flooded her face.

'Surely a real marriage would have been easier,' she muttered to herself as she stomped back to the bed. The couple would have been intimate beforehand—in most cases at least—but this business thing was proving difficult.

She found one of the pretty Thai night-dresses, took off her underwear and pulled it on, then climbed into the massive bed, refusing to think of other women with whom he might have shared it.

This was a business arrangement.

But in spite of her angst, she was all but asleep when she felt the mattress move, and Alex's long arm reached out and drew her close so he could spoon around her.

'We're both far too tired tonight, but I'll make it up to you tomorrow,' he whispered into her ear, then he nestled in beside her and she fell asleep to the sound of his breathing growing deeper and slower as he, too, fell asleep.

* * *

She woke, confused at first, then remembered where she was, Alex now sprawled on his back beside her, sound asleep still.

She crept out of bed, went to the bathroom, then quietly crossed the room to open the dark curtains just a crack so she could see what lay beyond the room.

It was eight o'clock local time, but the street-lights were still lit, and a faint fog made the buildings seem to float above the ground.

So this was Edinburgh!

Lovely old buildings stretching out along the opposite side of the street, no doubt matched by the one she was in. They were joined, and very stately, with painted front doors and small shrubs of some kind in painted pots on either side of the few steps that led up to the doors.

An urge to be out there, looking about, exploring, was almost enough to take her over to the wardrobe to start pulling on clothes, but Alex's arrival stopped her, his arms scooping her up.

'This is far too early for Edinburgh to wake up. You can go exploring all you want later in the day.'

He carried her across the room and she laughed as he all but dumped her on the bed, climbing on top of her to give her a hearty kiss on the lips.

'Welcome to Edinburgh,' he said, and proceeded to show her just how welcome she was.

For Edinburgh or for him? she wondered much later, when she'd regathered her senses after some tumultuous lovemaking and was enjoying a coffee and croissant that he'd brought in and placed by the bed.

Then he'd sat, bent and kissed her again, before becoming Mr Efficient, setting down some money, his address and two phone numbers, a map of the inner city—'I doubt you'll get much further in your explorations today'—and finally a credit card.

'The pin number is on the map so don't lose it,' he said. 'I'm sorry I can't show you around but there is still so much to do.'

She touched his face, and said, 'Go, do what you have to!'

She'd have liked to add, 'And I don't need your money or your credit card,' but she thought it might upset him, and he had enough on his plate at the moment.

Best she leave them both behind. She had the map Robert had given her, marked with the shops she might like to visit, her own credit card and money she could exchange for the local currency.

Once dressed, she checked her phone.

She had sent a long text to her father from the plane, and had tried to ring him the previous evening, but they would still be mustering and he was probably out at one of the camps.

She'd try again tonight.

It was four days later that she woke to the realisation that she had fallen in love with Alexander Monroe McLeod! Had probably loved him for some time.

It wasn't that she was seeing more of him, he was as busy as ever, and the conversations they did have over an occasional dinner or breakfast suggested that his gran's estate was large and convoluted.

The funeral was coming up—a trip to somewhere north, very far north and very cold, he'd told her, adding that the church was always freezing.

They'd drive, not fly, maybe take their time

driving back if she'd like that, although at this time of year fog and the thin mist Alex called haar would probably spoil any view.

Forewarned, Kenzie pulled out her warmest underwear and the boots she'd found herself on one of her expeditions into the beautiful city. For the funeral she'd wear the grey cashmere dress and dark blue coat, thick black stockings and her boots.

Long underwear, slacks, jumpers and the thick tweed coat should do for the trip, as she'd need to be able to peel off layers when she was inside.

Alex's car was a sleek, black saloon, immeasurably comfortable. For what seemed like hours they drove through the city, suburbs, maybe small towns that had been consumed by the city—built-up areas with plenty of traffic.

Ring roads with numbers on them seemed to weave back and forth, the traffic still thick.

A fine, misty rain made conditions even more difficult, so Kenzie could sit back and take in the view of the different style of buildings they were passing, enjoy the occasional patches of green, until, at last, they were on a narrower freeway, with less traffic and what seemed like endless fields rolling towards mist-shrouded mountains.

'It looks as if it would be beautiful if the mist cleared,' she said, and Alex turned with a quick smile.

'That's hardly ever,' he said, and she thought he might be joking, but wasn't sure.

They stopped for a break occasionally, each time, as she clambered out of the warm car, Kenzie was glad for Robert's advice, for even through her layers, the chill pierced her skin.

'Here at last!' Alex eventually said, pulling the car off the rough country lane they'd been on through tall stone pillars and onto a gravel drive that seemed to stretch to infinity.

Or somewhere into the mist!

'You go on inside while I get the bags,' Alex told her, and Kenzie hurried up the stone steps and was pleased to find Robert there to welcome her into a vast space, hung with portraits of ancestors, whether Alex's or someone else's, and, yes, a suit of armour near the bottom of each of the wide stairways that clung to the side walls...

Thank heaven for Robert!

Did he have the ability to be in two places at once?

It was only with great effort she held back the hug she'd have liked to give him or his doppelganger, for the journey had turned into a seemingly endless odyssey with who knew what at the end.

Alex breezed in, wisps of mist clinging to his clothing.

'Staff in place, everything in order?' he asked Robert, who assured him all was well.

And as if to prove it, Robert beckoned to someone behind him, and a couple of young women appeared. Neatly dressed in slacks and black tops—fortunately for Kenzie's composure not in dinky maid uniforms—they smiled a welcome.

'Millie and Mairi,' Robert said. 'They'll take the bags up and see everything's ready in the rooms. You'd like a drink to take off the chill, sir?'

And although Kenzie was surprised by the 'sir', it was obvious Alex had barely noticed, if at all.

'Whisky would be great, Robert. Kenzie,

what about you? Gin and tonic, or dare you try Scottish beer?'

'I do have some mulled wine. I thought Kenzie might find it warming,' Robert said, before Kenzie had to make a choice.

And at least Robert was still treating her as herself—she'd definitely be put out to be called madam, if that's what went with sir for females in posh houses.

For as Robert drew them from the entrance into a small drawing room—more portraits but hung this time on beautiful wallpapered walls, stripes of crimson, alternating with rose vines—she realised what this definitely was—a very posh house.

She thought of the big rambling old house she called home—always dusty, impossible to keep clean. It was considered something special as Outback houses went, but this?

Could it be a castle?

Alex took her arm and led her towards a chair by the big open fire, easing off her coat as they moved.

'Gran was up to date enough to have installed air-conditioning into a lot of this old pile, but somehow fires make things homely.'

'Homely?' Kenzie said with a grin, and he shrugged.

'We only use a few of the rooms. Most of them are closed off except in summer for a few open-house days.'

So even before DocSays, her husband hadn't been short of money. Though it wasn't his probable wealth that bothered Kenzie—she had plenty of her own—but the place itself, his position in it, his being at ease in it while to her it was totally alien.

She had no doubt that she could, in time, make herself fit into it, in her own way, of course, and maybe for parts of every year, but was it what she wanted?

Only if it came with love.

The thought came out of nowhere, *and* before she'd even sipped the mulled wine Robert had pressed into her hand.

She did sip now, and studied Alex as she enjoyed the warm, delicately spiced drink. He was talking to Robert about the funeral arrangements but she didn't want to listen, she wanted to look at him.

Look at him and try to work out when love had entered the arrangement between them—

when she'd stupidly forgotten it was a business arrangement and fallen in love...

Although, if she thought seriously about it, it had probably started way back at the island, when she'd been attracted to him from the start. Then the talk of a convenient marriage—while it had excited her nerves and set the blood pounding through her veins, she'd damped down the feelings by reminding herself it wasn't that kind of marriage.

And given that he was so insistent that Monroes didn't do emotion, she'd shut those feelings away rather than embarrass them both!

CHAPTER ELEVEN

THOUGH THIS HOUSE appeared to be as isolated as her own property back home, the funeral was extremely well attended. Kenzie eventually gave up on any attempt to remember names, hoping that those who were important to Alex and the family would go back to the house for food and drinks.

They'd have to go somewhere or remain in a frozen tableau around the grave.

'You're cold, I'll get Robert to take you home,' Alex said, taking hold of her gloved but still frozen hand.

'But shouldn't I stay?' she asked half-heartedly, already regretting the purchase of the stylish boots when she should have bought something with warm lining.

'No, they'll think you need to see to the arrangements.'

He dropped a kiss on her cheek and steered

her towards Robert, who stood, stiffly aloof at the head of the grave.

And one look at Robert's face was enough to tell Kenzie it was for Robert's sake as well as hers that Alex was sending them home, for the grief on his features made her want to cry for him.

Once at the car, she refused the back seat, and climbed into the front beside him, sliding across the acreage of seat, to rest her hand on his arm.

'This must be terribly hard for you,' she said, and saw the slightest of nods.

'You were with her a long time?' Kenzie asked gently.

'Man and boy,' Robert replied, and she could hear the pride in his voice. 'Were but a stable lad in the beginning, but learned the house from the bottom to the top.'

He paused before adding, 'And a finer woman you would never meet!'

Kenzie could hear the soft Scottish burr in his voice beneath the carefully cultivated language of the butler who would put aside his grief, check that all was in order for the funeral feast, and be there to greet the guests when they returned.

Heard grief, too, and hoped that somewhere there was someone to comfort *him*.

Back at the house he saw her to the door, sent someone to put away the car, and suggested she take off her coat and change into dry shoes.

She looked at the line of wellingtons, and outside boots neatly stored in a large cupboard off the entrance hall, and realised life wasn't all that different from back home.

Apart from the weather—and the butler, of course—but in her mind's eye she could see all the work boots lined up in the big hall at home, and for a moment felt very, very homesick…

Alex watched Kenzie and Robert drive away, and felt a sense of loss. She'd done no more than stand beside him, staunchly upright in this foreign setting, murmuring thanks for condolences when required, acknowledging introductions.

Yet now an unfamiliar ache in his chest suggested that he missed her.

He turned his attention resolutely back to the family and friends coming forward to speak to him, assuring all they'd be welcome back at the hall, suggesting they all needed something to counter the chill of the day.

Gran's solicitor touched his arm, suggesting a meeting later in the week, and with a pang he realised he'd have to consider the future of this estate—the Monroe estate—where he'd spent every Christmas and school holiday in his youth.

He spoke to a few stragglers, villagers who'd hung back but who had loved Gran as much as he had, for she had been their champion in all things.

No, he probably couldn't sell the estate...

He hadn't realised how much Kenzie had helped until, with all the guests departed, and everything set to rights by the army of helpers Robert had produced, he saw her slumped in a big chair in front of the fire, her usually bright face white with fatigue.

'You didn't have to stay—you could have gone up to the bedroom much earlier,' he scolded.

'It didn't seem right,' she said. 'Besides, everyone was busy and I doubt I'd have found my way.'

'You ask someone,' he said firmly, upset that she'd stoically stayed on, upset he hadn't thought to look out for her and see her taken up to bed.

She was sleeping soundly when he finally got up to bed, and, as exhaustion claimed him, he climbed in beside her, reached out one hand to rest it against her shoulder, and fell asleep.

He slept until the sun, that rarely seen star in the northern sky in winter, was bright behind a fine crack in the curtains.

No Kenzie, and the stab of disappointment he'd felt was probably because he'd have liked her to be there, to have held her, made love to her…

'She's out walking,' Robert informed him, 'but I told her you'd want to drive back today so she won't stay out long.'

'Far too cold for a tropical flower anyway,' he said to Robert, who surprisingly had his own comment to make.

'I doubt a little thing like the cold would daunt Miss Kenzie. I'll get your breakfast, sir.'

'Enough of the "sir", Robert,' Alex told him.

'We've lived without it for the past month or more, so surely we don't need it now.'

But Robert had glided off on silent feet before Alex had reached the end of his objection.

He sighed.

Robert had cared for his dying grandmother as gently as a nurse, but she'd always been madam to him, and probably always would be in his memories of her.

How strange Kenzie would have found it all, yet she'd never betrayed the slightest hint of discomfort or uncertainty.

He'd chosen well in this marriage of convenience, he decided, then laughed at the absurdity of the thought.

Had he had a choice?

She'd been right there, wanting the same thing he had—marriage!

It was the fact that they were well suited—in bed at least—that was the greatest discovery.

And again, for a moment, he wished she'd stayed in bed...

Walking in borrowed gumboots through the silent, misty morning had brought a sense of great peace to Kenzie.

The place had a feeling of vastness—nothing but moor and mountains as far as she could see.

Not that that was very far!

But she'd felt at home in the silence—it spoke of home—so she'd walked, always keeping the huge old house in sight, brighter now the sun was burning off the mists.

She'd go back to Edinburgh with Alex and talk to him there, tell him she was going home.

She'd been up at six, pulling on her coat and creeping from the dark bedroom to sit downstairs beside the dying embers of the fire in the small drawing room, computer in hand as she worked out how to fly from Edinburgh to Darwin with the shortest possible layover between flights.

It was a task that had seemed impossible at first, going from one international airline to another, until she'd gone to a site that compared flights and prices—not for the cost of the trip home but for the length of the journey.

Once she was away from here she wanted to be home as quickly as possible.

So she'd booked what she'd found—out of Edinburgh tomorrow and back in Darwin just over twenty-five hours later. She'd let her father know from Dubai, the first stop on the way, and he'd meet her so she'd be back on Spec a matter of hours later.

And you're glad—it will be wonderful, she told herself, but doubted herself would agree any time soon.

She made her way back to the house to find Alex up and apparently waiting for her.

'I'm sorry to be in a rush but there's so much to do and I really want to go back to work next week.'

He held her arm to steady her as she pulled off her gumboots, and she knew she shouldn't be excited by such a practical touch, but of course she was.

Excited and saddened.

'Did you enjoy your walk?' he asked, all politeness when what she really wanted was for him to drag her upstairs into the bedroom and—

Well, that wasn't going to happen.

'I've asked Robert to organise a flask of coffee and some sandwiches for the trip back. He said you had some tea and toast before you went out, do you want anything more substantial before we leave?'

She looked into the face she'd really just begun to know, and read his concern.

And something else?

Confusion?

Alex confused?

She scoffed at the thought, and hurried up to the bedroom to gather her things—*and* put on her boots!

She'd have to visit Melbourne in winter every year for the next ten years to get full value out of the clothes she'd bought, but as she packed them away she knew she was thinking flippant thoughts to keep her mind from what lay ahead.

Somehow—sleeping for a large part of it—she got through the journey back to Edinburgh.

Robert had been left behind to see to things on the estate—yes, she *had* listened to the conversations after the funeral, or some of them at least.

Dinner had once again been delivered magically to the door—not burgers and chips but chicken à la King in crispy pastry cases, cooked to perfection, with scalloped potatoes and carrots and peas. Bread and butter pudding to follow!

'It was my favourite on school holidays,' Alex said. 'Do you like it?'

He sounded anxious, so she assured him she did, but the look of anxiety lingered.

'I'm not going to be much fun to be with for a few days,' he said finally. 'The legal people want everything sorted as soon as possible, so it will be meetings, meetings and more meetings.'

Anxious again as he said, 'You won't mind exploring on your own?'

She set down her spoon, unable to eat any more, although it was the most delicious bread and butter pudding she'd ever tasted.

'Actually, Alex, I need to talk to you about that.'

He began to speak but she held up her hand, determined to get it all said.

'I hope you won't feel you cheated your grandmother, because it isn't you, it's me,' she began, then realised that didn't make much sense if you didn't know what came next.

She hurried on.

'You see, when I married you I was absolutely certain that this kind of business arrangement would suit me fine. That I could do it without any concerns, even enjoy it because you seemed like a nice guy.'

'Well, I'm glad you at least thought that.' Very stilted—very Alexander Monroe McLeod!

Best get it over with.

'Yes, well, the thing is I've discovered I can't do it—do a business marriage—and I'm sorry to let you down, and I'm happy to pay all the costs of a divorce, but I've realised I want a different kind of marriage.' She could feel the heat flooding her cheeks, but soldiered on. 'One where I can love and be loved.' She hesitated for a moment, then said, 'There—that's all. I've booked a flight home tomorrow, so I'll just go and pack.'

She fled—no other word for it—getting out of that room so quickly she had to pause to catch her breath before tackling the stairs in front of her.

Gobsmacked didn't begin to cover Alex's reaction. He sat, staring at the door through which his wife had disappeared, battling to understand exactly what she'd said.

He'd been so pleased with his marriage—with his *wife*! So happy they were compatible in bed, so filled with admiration for her when she'd been thrown into a massive social occasion at the funeral—proud as Punch really!

And now she was gone.

Well, going, but with a flight booked and not a word to him!

He should feel angry or at the very least aggrieved but the tightness in his gut wasn't either of those emotions.

Not that he knew *what* it was…

And he had meetings with the lawyers all day tomorrow so wouldn't be able to take her to the airport.

And he was thinking this because…?

He shook his head, trying to clear it, trying to work out if there was something he could do.

But it *had* been a business arrangement—a marriage of convenience—so could he in all good faith complain that she wanted to leave?

Yet more than anything he wanted to hold her in his arms and make things right between them again.

In *bed*! A voice inside his head scoffed. Hasn't she just told you that's not enough…?

CHAPTER TWELVE

LEAVING WITHOUT SAYING goodbye to Robert had been harder than she'd realised, which was why, she told herself, she was sitting in the taxi, crying as quietly as she could, not wanting to attract the attention of the driver.

But it was the only way! she reminded herself.

To stay in the marriage, now she knew she loved Alex, would be agony.

She had no doubt he liked her well enough, and they were certainly good together in bed, but her heart would always want to hear words of love, and, as Alex had told her many times, Monroes didn't do emotion.

Yet he'd loved his grandmother, she knew that—knew from the way he'd looked at her, the gentle way he'd taken her fragile hand. Knew from the feeling in every word as he'd read to her—yes, he did feel emotion for all his denial.

Just not for her, and why should she expect it? She'd known what she was getting into.

Had even *thought* it a good idea!

Well, it *had* been, compared to the difficulty of internet dating when you lived in the middle of nowhere...

No, falling in love with him had been her own fault—well, partly his for being such a—a fine man, she decided was the only apt description.

How could she not have fallen for him?

Done what had seemed impossible—unthinkable—when she'd first agreed to his proposition.

And even though she'd married him with the idea of having children, she'd discovered she couldn't live with him without love—without being loved...

Edinburgh airport wasn't nearly as vast as London's Heathrow, but anything bigger than Darwin's international terminal seemed vast to her.

And confusing, although that was good as she had to think about finding her way to the right departure lounge and didn't have time to think about Alex.

Unfortunately, for the twenty-five hours and

twenty minutes after boarding her first flight, she'd have plenty of time for that particular reflection.

Although, with stops in Dubai and Singapore, and perhaps a sleep on each flight, and food—they always fed you on international flights—

She stopped in the middle of the main concourse to pull herself together, to have a stern talk to herself about the practicalities of what she was doing, and the uselessness of regrets.

With renewed determination, she studied the departures board, joined a long queue to check in her luggage—one heavily packed backpack—found her way through security to where she had to be, and finally settled into a comfortable business-class seat in the giant aircraft.

She accepted the glass of champagne handed to her pre-take-off, drank it, and closed her eyes, not wanting to see the famous old city from the air, not wanting to think...

Alex hoped he was making all the correct responses to the lawyers' talk. They certainly didn't seem to sense there was anything wrong with him.

Well, there wasn't, was there?

He wasn't sick, he wasn't worried about work or money, or even what to have for his dinner. Wasn't worried about anything.

Except his wife had left him, which didn't, he realised, precisely *worry* him as cause him a strange kind of disconnectedness.

Not a good state to be in when talking— or more listening—to lawyers. But he knew how everything in Gran's estate would be bequeathed and to whom. He'd known for years, had read every change in her will, so really did he need to be here?

He'd have to sign things, of course, but they could be sent to him.

He'd decided the previous evening, when the fact of Kenzie's departure had sunk in, that he'd be able to handle this interminable meeting with Gran's—and his—lawyers. After all, Monroes didn't do emotion.

So why was his mind throwing up gruesome images of plane wrecks, intermingled with images of her beautiful body resting beside him, her sleepy smile as they drew apart after making love—

'Alex!'

The word was sharp enough for him to realise it wasn't the first time this person had spoken it.

'Sorry,' he said, 'it's been a hectic few days.'

'Hectic couple of weeks, from the sound of things,' William—he thought it was William—said. Lawyers all seemed to look the same to him—maybe it was the pin-striped suits and sober ties…

'Archie was asking about your will now you're married. You'll want to change it, won't you? If you give us just a rough idea of what you'd like, we can get on with it while we're doing the transfer of your grandmother's bequests into your name.'

Alex stared blankly at William—he was almost certain it *was* William—at a total loss as to a reply.

I'm not married any more, sounded stupid, besides which, saying it out loud would make it more real, and—

And what?

And he didn't want it to be real, he realised. He very much didn't want it to be real!

'Let's just get Gran's estate settled first,' he finally said, because his mind was in more turmoil than ever now he'd figured the 'real' thing out.

William, or maybe Archie, said something, but he knew he didn't want to be in that office a moment longer. He wanted to be at the airport, finding his wife, talking to her, trying to work out what the hell had gone wrong...

'Do you know if there are any direct flights from here to Darwin?'

'Darwin, Australia?' one of them asked, but, lawyer-like, he woke the laptop sitting on his desk and began to search.

'None direct,' he said. 'There are multiple ways to get there, all with at least two stop-overs and flight changes as far as I can see. Is she from Darwin, your wife?'

He turned the laptop so Alex could see the list of flights that would eventually take Kenzie back to Australia.

And would she even fly into Darwin?

Would that be the closest to her home?

Archie was asking something, but Alex

barely heard his voice, his mind grappling with the fact that he knew so little about his wife.

But he did know the phone number!

He looked back at the list of flights again, searching to see when she'd be expected to land in Darwin—

If she was going to Darwin.

He stood up.

'Sorry, but I need to go. You both know what to do, and anything that needs a signature can wait until I get back.'

'Get back?' they echoed in unison.

'From Australia,' he told them, and left the room.

Logistics—it was just a matter of logistics. He had no idea if one of the charter planes he used when travelling could fly that far without refuelling, or even with one pilot, but one phone call to the company and all that would be sorted.

It would be hot in Australia, possibly even hotter than Thailand, but he had lightweight clothes from his stay there, and jeans—he was pretty sure jeans would be the thing he'd need. He'd go back to the flat, organise a flight, pack and be ready to go whenever they had a plane available.

As he hurried down the corridor his mind was already on that plane, travelling out to a place with fifteen thousand head of cattle...

And one lithe and lovely dark-haired woman!

The interminable flight finally landed in Dubai, where Kenzie, totally lost as far as time was concerned, phoned her father.

'I'm coming home,' she said succinctly. 'ETA Darwin two-thirty tomorrow afternoon. That's if tomorrow is Thursday out there.'

'Are you okay?' her father asked, and she assured him she was before telling him they were calling her flight and she had to go. Any explanation—worse, any kindness from her father—and she'd have burst into tears in the middle of one of the world's busiest airports.

She'd left the lounge to find a quiet corner to phone her father, but now returned, working her way down the array of food choices but not tempted by any.

Maybe a cold beer. They had Coopers, which her father favoured, so it would give her a taste of home.

But a phone call and cold beer did little to repel the thought that maybe she'd made a mistake.

Just maybe, getting on a plane and flying home had been a stupid thing to do—irrational even, and she was not an irrational person.

They could have talked, but what was there to talk about in a business arrangement?

Besides which, Alex had already said he'd be tied up with lawyers all day, and possibly the next day too, and she knew he was hoping to get back to work the following week.

And from what she knew of emergency room doctors, there'd be little chance of talking after that.

No, it was the best thing to do—get out of there and begin to put her life back together again.

This she was confident of doing, though putting her heart back together...

An attendant came to tell her the flight to Singapore was boarding and she thanked her warmly, glad to have something definite to do—something to think about apart from Alex.

A pre-take-off champagne and she'd close her eyes and sleep. No turning back now.

But once in her seat, she did check her phone before turning it to flight mode.

No message from Alex, and why would there be?

Business arrangements broke down all the time and, given the extent of his own wealth and his gran's estate, he'd have to know a lot about business.

She drank her champagne, and closed her eyes. Once at Singapore she was almost home…

Apparently, it was relatively easy for a private jet to fly to Australia.

'No worries, mate,' the man he'd spoken to said. 'I'll come myself. Need a trip home.'

Further questioning told him they'd use three pilots and have a short stopover in Abu Dhabi.

'When do you want to leave?' the obliging man asked.

'Whenever you're organised,' Alex said, feeling what could only be excitement somersaulting in his stomach.

'Let's say six tomorrow morning. You've used us before, you know where to go?'

Half statement, half question.

'I'll be there,' Alex assured him, wondering

at the same time whether his newfound Aussie pilot knew much about the place where they were headed.

'Up the gulf,' Kenzie had said, which hadn't meant much to Alex until he'd found a map of Australia online and seen the huge gulf at the top of it, and the vast amounts of land around said gulf.

A different excitement stirred inside him now. To be going somewhere new, somewhere entirely different.

How had his life become so proscribed, so work-focussed, that he'd never so much as considered seeing more of the world?

He'd never have got as far as a small island in the Gulf of Thailand had it not been for Gran.

Never met Kenzie.

Never—

What?

Fallen in love?

He wasn't entirely certain that's what it had been, just that being with her was unlike any other connection he'd ever had with a woman.

And being without her—the prospect of being without her for ever—unbearable…

CHAPTER THIRTEEN

'WHERE ARE YOU going after Darwin, mate?' the Aussie pilot, Tom, asked when he came back to sit with Alex on the last leg of the flight.

'A property called Speculation, somewhere up the gulf, I believe.'

'Wow!' the pilot said. 'That's some place! One of the biggest in Australia, I've heard.'

There was silence for a few minutes, no doubt while he considered Alex's destination, then he said, 'Why are you flying into Darwin? Some-one meeting you there?'

'No, but I understood it was the closest major airport.'

'It is that,' Tom told him. 'But Spec's got a good airstrip. RFDS—that's the Flying Doc-tors—put down there for a regular clinic every couple of weeks. Same size plane as this. Ac-tually, same model—well, some of the planes are the same model. It's a while since I flew for them.'

It took Alex a minute or two to make sense of this conversation in his head.

'You can land on the property?'

'Sure can. I'll have to get on to them to let them know we're coming, although they're such a big place they don't have to move stray cattle off the runway like some of the places do.'

Moving cattle off the runway?

Clinic runs?

Increasingly intrigued by this glimpse into what Kenzie's life must have been like, Alex had to ask.

'What are clinic runs?'

Tom smiled at him.

'Hard to get your head around our Outback,' he said. 'A clinic run is going out to do a few hours, maybe a day, at a specific place—very small settlements like some of the opal mining towns or a property somewhere. People come a hundred, two hundred k to see the doc. It's like your GP has moved into town for the day, and you make appointments, kids get vaccinated, pregnant mums checked, older people might have issues—diabetes is common.'

'So once a fortnight the service flies a doctor—'

'And nurses,' Tom put in. 'Sometimes a dentist.'

'A team, then, out to this property to see whoever needs a bit of medical care or treatment for ongoing issues. I knew of the service but thought they mainly attended accidents in rural locations—emergency stuff like an ambulance. It's unbelievable!'

'Not really, mate,' Tom said. 'They do the emergency stuff, all right, and risky that can be. But the regular clinic service has been going on for decades now. People out in the bush rely on it. You want a coffee? Something to eat?'

As Tom departed to fix a snack in the small kitchen, Alex battled to make sense of what he'd heard. He'd always known Australia was a vast land, but he'd somehow imagined all that space in the middle of it was empty, not dotted with properties as big as Scotland, or tiny opal mining settlements.

And the more he learned, the more he wanted to know. Somewhere in the mists of time, he'd seen Kenzie taking their children—why only two?—back to Australia from time to time, maybe staying a month or so, but he'd be busy at work. It had seemed a sensible arrangement.

Until, of course, he'd realised that he couldn't last twenty-four hours without Kenzie, let alone a month or two. And, given that life-shattering discovery, he now thought he'd probably miss his children too.

Children he didn't have—might never have…

No! That was plain impossible.

He'd see Kenzie, talk to her—she was the most pragmatic woman he'd ever met—and together they'd work things out.

Kenzie positively bounced out of the plane at Darwin, excited to be home. And if she was sick at heart, well, that was for her to know— her and only her.

Once through customs, the tall, rangy figure of her father in his daggy, wide-brimmed hat brought a few tears to her eyes, but she hid them against his shirt as they hugged each other.

He took her backpack from her, linked his arm through hers, and said, 'I've brought the chopper—we'll be home in no time.'

'Had you finished the muster or am I being a nuisance?' she asked, and he squeezed her hand.

'You could never be a nuisance but, yes,

we've finished the muster, you'll see the road trains full of cattle heading for here as we fly home.'

They walked the kilometre to the private section of the airport, Kenzie asking questions to keep her father talking.

Talk about cattle numbers and expected sales figures was easier than enquiries about her marriage or what she was doing home.

Her dad wouldn't ask—he never had—apparently firmly convinced that in her own sweet time Kenzie would tell him what was bothering her.

It's how they'd always worked, from the time when she had been little and had seen one of the manager's bigger boys teasing the dogs. She'd had to weigh up telling tales, which she knew wasn't right, and the dogs' welfare, and had eventually chosen the dogs, although that boy had called her a tittle-tat for months afterwards.

'So, given the drought and the floods, how bad or good were the numbers?' she asked, because now she'd remembered that she'd had quite a crush on that boy a few years later, and didn't really want to think about that either...

Her father talked her through the muster figures.

'We saved all the breeding stock from the floods—already had them in the hill paddock. Lost one of the good bulls, but the Ainsworths have a beauty they're wanting to sell.'

It was normal, everyday chat and Kenzie felt it like a soothing balm spread across her body. She was nearly home—everything would be fine.

As her father filed his flight plan, she bought some bottled water, then she was in the air again and, no, she wasn't going to cry, but as they grew closer to the cluster of buildings that was home, her father patted her knee and said, 'We'll be right, lass. We'll get through this.'

'What the hell?'

She'd been busy mopping up tears, so hadn't seen the strange aircraft on the runway until her father's exclamation.

She peered at it—no insignia...

'It's not RFDS,' she said.

'And not been here long—dust not settled yet,' her father said. 'That's one of the lads going out in the ute to meet it.'

The chopper slowed, then gracefully dropped

down onto the pad close to the house, the strange plane now a distant glimmer.

'He must be taking off again that he's stopped down there, not taxied to the house,' her father said, but the sight of her so-familiar home, the big house, with the smaller buildings clustered around it like chicks around the mother hen, had brought fresh tears to her eyes.

Wayne, their foreman for many years, was there to help her down, giving her a hug to welcome her home.

'Pleased to see the old place, eh?" he said, one lean brown finger wiping a tear from her cheek.

'You bet!' she said, because that would be expected of her.

And being home *was* good.

It was home! A place to heal, with time and space to build her life again.

'Apparently, the bloke on that fancy jet's here to see you,' Wayne continued. 'Ute's on its way over now.'

He pointed to the dust trail behind the very dusty vehicle.

Bloke on a fancy jet?

It was the only way Alex ever travelled.

Her stomach turned over and her heart leapt,

but she told herself it was more likely to be one of the lawyers.

Her father was standing beside her—Wayne on one side, Dad on the other—unknowingly giving her the strength to face whoever got out of the ute.

'Mr Steele?' Alex said, as, immaculately dressed in chinos and a short-sleeved blue shirt, he stepped out into the dust and held out his hand. 'I'm Alex McLeod.'

Her father shook hands, saying, 'You've come to check us out?'

Alex shook his head, then turned to Kenzie.

'I've come to see Kenzie,' he said, and reached out to take her two hands, which were hanging limply on the end of her arms as she tried to get over the shock of what was happening.

'What with my grandmother's funeral and all the travel, there's a lot of things we didn't get around to saying to each other.'

'Kenzie?' her father said, in a voice that asked if she was all right with this.

'I'm fine, Dad,' she managed, although she knew she really, really wasn't.

Why was he here?

Surely he hadn't come to discuss divorce!

All of that could be handled over the net.

'Why don't you take Alex up to the homestead, out on the side veranda is cool at this
time of the day, and I'll send Maggie out with
cold drinks,' her father said, apparently realising she'd been struck dumb *and* unable to
move.

'You'd like a beer, Mr McLeod?'

Whoops!

Her father clearly thought Alex was up to no
good, arriving like this. The iron in his voice
suggested he'd guessed she was a mess, and he
only had one person to blame.

'Call him Alex,' she managed, and felt those
long slim fingers that had traced her body and
brought her such pleasure in bed tighten on
hers, just briefly.

'Side veranda,' her father repeated, and
stalked away towards the house.

But Wayne was still there, and would remain,
Kenzie knew, until she assured him she was
okay.

'This way,' she said to Alex, detaching one
hand so she could lead him through the gate

into the garden, and around the shrubs to the side veranda.

Which got rid of Wayne, but left her with Alex...

'Some place,' he said, waving his arm in the general direction of the other houses and out-buildings.

She snatched her hand away.

'What are you doing here?' she demanded. 'Did you come to check out where I live? Some place, is it? Not what you expected? A tin shed maybe!'

'Kenzie!'

His voice was soft, and shaking slightly.

He put his hand on her shoulder and turned her towards him.

'I've come to tell you I love you,' he said, blurting out the words as if saying them slowly might be impossible.'

He touched her cheek.

'Love you and want to be loved by you,' he said, his voice rough now. 'I came to find out if I could be that man you wanted to be married to—the one you could love and be loved by.'

Kenzie stared at him in total disbelief.

This was Alex—Alex 'Monroes don't do

emotion' Alex. Standing in the shrubbery, telling her he loved her.

Well, she thought that's what he was telling her.

'Where are you, Kenzie? I've brought drinks but first get yourself up here so I can give you a hug, girl. The old place is a mausoleum without you around.'

'That's Maggie, with drinks,' Kenzie said to Alex.

He smiled and answered, 'On the side veranda. We'd better go.'

And, Alex-like, he took control, steering her along the path, up the three steps and onto the side veranda, where she let go of his hand for long enough to give Maggie a hug, and introduce her to Alex.

'This the husband, then?' Maggie said. 'How come he comes on a fancy jet and you had to fly commercial?'

This really wasn't the best place to try to sort out why Alex was here. Too many protectively inquisitive people around—too many people who loved her and were loved by her.

So, rather than answer Maggie, she turned to the man in question.

'Did you mean what you said just then—about loving and being loved by?'

He half smiled.

'Of course!' he said. 'Have I ever said anything to you I didn't mean?'

Had he?

She couldn't think.

But if he had said that—

'You love me?' she asked, just to be sure.

'And why wouldn't he?' Maggie demanded huffily.

'I do,' Alex said, and drew her closer, to show her just how much in a kiss that stole her breath.

Kenzie broke away eventually, reasonably sure Maggie had stayed to witness most of it.

She'd be reporting back to the men in the kitchen that everything was all right with their girl, and any minute her father would join them on the veranda.

She led Alex to one of the low-slung, wood and canvas chairs, and sat in one beside him, reaching out for a cold stubby of beer, handing him a cooler to put it in.

'Aussie pub!' she said with a smile, and when

he touched her fingers as he took the beer, she knew everything was going to be all right.

'Can you stay?' she asked, and he smiled at her.

'As long as you'd like me to,' he said.

She had to laugh.

'You'd be bored silly after a couple of days and I thought you were itching to get back to work.'

Weird conversation when her internal conversationalist kept shouting, *He loves me!*

But most of the words she wanted to say and hear were best left to the privacy of their bedroom, probably in the bed Maggie would be making up for them right now!

'It's a bit late now, but tomorrow, if you can stay on, Kenzie'll show you around the place,' her father said, appearing on the veranda with his beer in his hand.

'You've just missed the muster—it's been hectic, so right now we're all taking a few days' break.'

There was a slight pause before he added, 'But if you're out in the western paddock, Kenz, you can check the bore there. I was going to do that today.'

'Until you had an SOS for a lift home.' Kenzie smiled at the man she loved most in the world, in fact, at both the men she loved most in the world.

And now Alex had relaxed enough to be asking questions of her father. How many people lived on the property? How did the cattle get to market? Was that Darwin, the market?

They had dinner, just the three of them, in the dining room, rather than the kitchen, Maggie producing steak tartare as an entrée, Kenzie guessing it was a test for Alex as well as one of her favourite foods.

'There'll be other things if you don't like it,' Kenzie said to Alex, but he ate with every appearance of enjoyment, complimenting Maggie when she returned to get their plates.

Roast beef, followed, rare and pink inside, perfect Yorkshire puddings to go with it, crisply baked potatoes, a sweet yam of some kind, and fresh cut beans.

'This food is magnificent,' Alex said, when Maggie returned with horseradish and mustard for the table.

'It's our own beef,' Maggie told him, 'so it's not that hard to get it right.'

'She's hiding her light under a bushel,' Kenzie teased, as Maggie turned to leave the room. 'Cooking is her passion and we've dined like royalty ever since Maggie took over the kitchen from the previous cook my grandmother had trained.'

'He's the one taught me about Yorkshire puddings,' Maggie admitted. 'He was a good cook, just getting old and tired.'

'Well, just make sure you're passing on your skills to one of the next generation,' Angus told her, and she beamed at him.

'Not the next, but the next. Young Tracy's mad about it! Always under my feet in the kitchen.'

'Tracy's one of Maggie's grandchildren, growing up here on the property. Her father's in charge of the horses.'

'Horses?' Alex turned to Angus. 'I'd have thought those bikes would have taken over most of the stock work.'

Her father nodded.

'They did, for a while, and we still use them to go around the boundaries, checking fences, things like that, but—'

'Dad's going back to the old ways.' Kenzie

finished for him. 'Using horses seems to keep the cattle calmer, mainly because calm cattle don't drop weight. We've even cut back on helicopter mustering, although we still use the choppers, flying higher, to find cattle that have wandered into the hills.'

'Hills?' Alex echoed weakly. 'From the air it looked as flat as this table.'

'That's more than enough for the poor chap to take in, Kenzie,' her father said quietly. 'Go for a drive tomorrow, show him the hills and the dams, give him more of an idea of the place.'

'I'd like that,' Alex said, 'but don't horses mean more—you call them stockmen?

'They do and we like it that way. During the big muster we bring in extra horsemen, but here on Spec we have up to a dozen at any one time.'

'They come and go,' Kenzie explained. 'Even the ones who grew up here.'

'Grew up here?'

Alex was aware he was beginning to sound like an echo, but this place was so much more than he'd expected. The food was as good as anything he'd ever eaten at one of Edinburgh's top restaurants.

And now it appeared there were other children apart from Kenzie who grew up here.

Kenzie took pity on him.

'We've always had two or three couples living here, their kids growing up here. When I was born, Maggie's youngest was three, so she kind of took me on as well.'

'Maggie's husband is the station manager now.' Angus took up the explanations. 'But back then he was head stockman, a job one of his sons does now.'

'And another of her sons is the property mechanic, working with one of our old mechanic's daughters in the big shed,' Kenzie said.

'And now we're confusing you,' Angus put in. 'Simply put, and you'll see a lot of it tomorrow, we usually have at least two married couples living here—three at the moment. And they all have children and sometimes the children stay on, or go away to learn a trade, or study and come back.'

'Our bookkeeper is one of the old mechanic's children and the teacher, Belle, is the eldest of Maggie's children.'

He couldn't help it—had to echo, 'Teacher?'

'Well, there are always kids to educate and

they mainly do School of the Air, but to have a trained teacher with them, helping out on all their lessons, is wonderful.'

Alex held up his hands in surrender.

'Don't tell me any more,' he said. 'My mind's already boggling at it all.'

Kenzie laughed—a sound he'd thought he'd never hear again. It warmed him all over.

'Think of it as a village in the country,' she said. 'Isolated but sufficient within itself. We even have a village shop.'

'Now you're teasing me,' he said, and she shook her head.

'We buy in bulk the staples like flour and sugar, butter and powdered milk, washing powder, soap—everything a shop might need. And everyone gets what they need when they need it. It only opens in the afternoon and usually one of the older kids works there.'

'Kenzie loved being in the shop, right from when she was little,' Angus told Alex.

And Kenzie added, 'We also get in treats like crisps and lollies. Soft drinks and beer, too.'

Astounded, Alex shook his head.

'I'll just have to wait and see,' he said, finishing his glass of the very acceptable burgundy Angus had produced to go with the beef.

'Come out and see the stars,' Kenzie said, getting to her feet. 'You'll excuse us, Dad.'

'Yes, go. You've both had a long day and should by rights be suffering terrible jet-lag.'

'Phooey to that—he needs to see the stars.'

And, Alex conceded, as he held Kenzie close to his side and looked up at the sky, he *had* needed to see the stars.

'There are more of them than I'd ever have believed possible,' he said quietly, so awed by the brilliant arc of starlit sky above him he could barely breathe.

'And they're here to give you their magic every night,' Kenzie said, turning to lead him back inside. 'Except in the wet, of course,' she added, and Alex dimly remembered her mentioning such a phenomenon once before.

There was so much for him to learn, it could take a lifetime.

And *that* thought planted a tiny seed somewhere deep inside him. He'd think about it later, but right now kissing Kenzie in the starlight seemed a better idea, kissing her in bed an even more exciting one.

He held her close, kissed her once, then turned back towards the house, the shadows of a few of what Kenzie had called house dogs trailing at their heels.

He had more questions later as they lay in bed, relaxed after making love, slowly and emotionally, saying with their bodies what their words had already said.

'Tell me about growing up here,' he said, and she leaned up on one elbow to kiss him on the lips.

'Tomorrow,' she said. 'You'll understand more when you've seen the place, but right now I need to sleep.'

He wrapped his arms around her and pulled her close, so she fell asleep to the sound of his voice, whispering about love.

CHAPTER FOURTEEN

THEY TOURED THE property the next day, taking
a ute rather than horses for both the air-conditioning and speed. Kenzie kept the bore in the
western paddock for last, because she knew
they'd be hot and tired by then.

'It's a lake,' Alex said in amazement as she
drew up by the bore that fed into the man-made
dam.

'And great for swimming,' she told him, when
she'd checked the bore and walked down to the
water's edge to join Alex, who was still amazed
to find this water in the arid land.

'Can we swim?'

Heat was pounding down on them, and Alex's
pale, Scottish skin was flushed with it.

'That's why we're here,' she said, and began
to strip off the worn cotton T-shirt and shorts
she'd been wearing, having to tug off her boots
first—boots and socks, shorts and shirt, bra

and panties soon lay in a neat heap on a large rock by the edge.

'Last one in's a dirty rat,' Kenzie challenged.

'But I've got more clothes on than you,' Alex protested.

But Kenzie was already in, breaststroking across the water, diving down out of sight and emerging with her hair slicked back from her head.

'My beautiful mermaid,' Alex said, when he emerged from below the water beside her.

He took her in his arms and kissed her, not an easy feat as the water was deep and they both had to keep their legs moving to stay afloat.

'You've blown me away—you know that, don't you?' he said, when they'd crossed the dam and were sitting on a rock on the other side. 'This place, the people, the space, the cattle—the sky! Even in the daytime it's just vast.'

Kenzie kissed him.

'That's nearly as good to hear as when you said you loved and wanted to be loved by me,' she told him, her heart still tripping at the memory of his words.

'I do, and I do,' he said, returning her kiss. 'Love you more than I could ever believe possible. I was sitting in this lawyers' boardroom with William and Archie and I couldn't make sense of a word they said, because my head was filled with you and—although this sounds strange—with the emptiness of not having you in my life. I've known both those men since I was at school, but I couldn't tell which was which because all the time my mind was on you.

'I thought I might catch you at the airport, mentioned flights to Darwin, and, probably realising I'd lost my mind, one of them brought up all the possibilities, and I knew I couldn't begin to guess how you'd travelled. So I excused myself, told then to send the papers to me to sign, and left, phoning the executive jet company as I went down in the lift.'

He kissed her again.

'Did I mention I loved you?'

'Many times,' she assured him, kissing him back. 'And I love you, more than words can ever say.'

Then somehow, on the hard slab of rock by the side of the dam, they were making love— urgently this time, needing affirmation of the words they'd spoken.

* * *

They swam again then drove back slowly, Kenzie showing him the machinery shed, the little school house—a school in miniature with computers on all the desks.

'It's how they talk to their teachers and the other kids,' Kenzie explained, but it was all too much to take in. He needed to think, to remember where they'd been and all that had been explained, then realised he'd need a lifetime to learn it all.

Well, he had a lifetime, didn't he?

Most of one…

Back at the homestead, Angus announced they were having a barbecue to welcome them both to Spec and celebrate their marriage.

It was held in a huge shed, hay bales for seats, a forty-four-gallon drum cut in half lengthwise to provide the base for a fire, an iron grill to throw the meat onto.

Other drums held ice with bottles of wine and 'stubbies'—small-sized bottles of beer—sticking out of it. Long tables were laid out with appetisers and salads, and kids scampered around in the dirt, swung from trees outside the shed, climbed the hay bales, and generally had a great time.

It was a totally foreign atmosphere, yet he felt relaxed.

Happy?

Definitely—especially with Kenzie by his side...

But it felt more than that. The place intrigued him and the people surrounding them—so open in their delight to have Kenzie back amongst them—

It was special to her and he could understand why...

She introduced him to all the adults, explaining who they all were. An old, gnarled-looking aboriginal stockman gave her a big hug, and tears rolled down both their cheeks as he said gruffly, 'Your mum would have been so pleased.'

'Bahlu came here with Mum when she married, from her parents' property down south. He was her spirit guardian, he always said, and then mine,' Kenzie explained, as Alex produced a handkerchief to dry her eyes.

They ate, had a glass of wine—another fine red that complemented perfectly cooked steaks—and sat on scratchy hay bales while people came to talk to them, to wish them well, to kiss Kenzie and hug her, more often than not.

He was halfway through a piece of pavlova filled with cream and passionfruit when a loud voice blaring from a speaker silenced the entire crowd.

'You there, Spec? Over,' it said, and he saw Wayne move to take up a small device that was obviously connected to a radio system.

'Spec here, go ahead.'

'Single vehicle RTA about fifteen k south on the Riverbend Road,' the disembodied voice said. 'Motorcyclist called it in on a cellphone and he's waiting by the vehicle. Says you might need to cut the two people out. RFDS alerted, they'll land on your strip as the road there's chewed up with all the road trains on the move.'

'Got it, Rob. We'll attend. Over and out.'

Alex turned to ask Kenzie what it all meant, but she was gone, already heading towards the big mechanics shed where most of the vehicles were garaged.

He followed.

If she was going out to this accident, so was he—after all, he *was* a doctor.

Arc lights lit the cavernous space and he found her and Wayne grabbing bags off a shelf and throwing them into the flat bed of a ute.

'I'll come,' he said, and she nodded, then ducked as Wayne went past him with what looked like the giant pincers of some prehistoric insect.

Aware he could only keep out of the way—these two obviously had their routine down pat—he began to look at what the ute already contained. Two large rectangular objects drew his attention and he turned his head to see what was written on the label on the side of the closest one.

Self-inflating airbed? On a rescue mission?

'In you get,' Kenzie said to him, apparently indifferent to road rules and safety regulations, Wayne climbed into the back of the vehicle and settled on top of one of the still-packed airbeds.

The engine was already running and the vehicle slowly moving off as Alex flung himself into the passenger seat, then they were off.

'You do this often?' he asked as the vehicle bumped over corrugations on a track he didn't know. Although it was dark beyond the headlights, so maybe he had been that way.

'You'll have to get the gates,' she said, and he realised she was so focussed on getting to where they were going she probably hadn't heard his question.

Twenty minutes later they pulled up beside the motorcyclist, whose battery was probably draining as he'd kept his headlight on so they could see him.

'I got the passenger out, and wrapped my jacket over her,' he said, 'but the driver's trapped. He's got a pulse.'

Kenzie thanked him, but Alex had already found the injured woman and was kneeling by her.

'Can't see much,' Alex said to Kenzie as she arrived by his side, bags slung over both shoulders.

Then suddenly the scene was lit by battery-operated arc lights Wayne had set up near the ute, and he could see not only the injured woman but the portable defibrillator that was one of the bags Kenzie had carried over.

'Do you want to check the driver?' she said to him. 'Wayne will be over there now with the cutters. I've got a fairly comprehensive medical kit in that other bag there. Take it in case you need it.'

The light was strong enough to reach the vehicle, and they could see the crumpled front end, and the engine block pushed back into the driver's side.

'If we can get the seat out with him in it, we can get a good look at him,' Wayne said. 'I've cut the seatbelt and moved it a couple of centimetres. Can you get that door open and look at what damage I might do if I move it more?'

Opening the door might have sounded easy but it took a great deal of physical levering with a short crowbar to actually detach it from the hinge end and pull it away.

But at least now he could examine the driver, who was unconscious but had a pulse, for all it was thin and thready.

'He's clear of the steering wheel,' he reported to Wayne, 'but the way the engine's come back has trapped his legs.'

He felt around with his hands, and found the wetness of blood. Lots of blood!

It seemed to be coming from his left thigh but there was no way he could tell for sure, and even if there had been, he was in no position to apply a bandage or tourniquet.

He shoved at the engine block, not intending to do the impossible and move it, but to see if it was likely to move if they attempted to get the man out.

Nothing.

'I think if we can get the seat out from under him, we'd be able to slide him out,' he told Wayne. 'Short of a crane arriving to lift the entire engine, I can't see any other option.'

Wayne looked around.

'Never a tree when you want one,' he muttered. 'We've got a winch and a good tow rope and could have tried it ourselves. But the seat's definitely moving and if we can both work at it we might get it looser. There's another small pinch bar—thing with a gooseneck—in the ute. If you grab that and get in the other side, we'll do this thing.'

Alex needed the pinch bar to get the other door open but once crouched inside he saw what Wayne was doing to release the seat from its anchors, and within minutes had it loose enough to cautiously lower it enough to slide it backwards.

'The girl's conscious. They'd had a fight! I've wrapped her in a blanket and left her with Steve—he's the motorcycle guy. What can I do?'

Kenzie had come over and was standing beside the car.

'Get a pad ready to staunch bleeding and bandages, a stethoscope if your travelling medical chest carries one,' Alex told her as the seat they'd been working on dropped and they were able to gently move the trapped man out from under the front of the vehicle.

Blood spurted from his left thigh and Alex clamped his hand over it.

'Find something we can use as a tourniquet on his thigh,' Alex said to Wayne, who within seconds had magicked up a professional mechanical tourniquet, which he wrapped around the victim's upper thigh and tightened.

'That's eased the flow,' Alex said, taking the pad Kenzie held out, then binding it tightly to the wound on the leg.

'Time check?' Kenzie said, and Wayne gave her the exact time he'd tightened the ligature.

'You two have done this before?' he said,

while his hands and eyes were checking out their patient for other injuries.

'Practised enough,' Wayne said laconically.

'Then do we splint his damaged ankle or leave that for the flying doctors when they arrive?

'Stabilise it,' Kenzie said. 'Even with the air-beds it's going to be a rough ride home for them.'

Alex was wondering just what they had available to do that when Wayne said, 'No pulse!'

And Kenzie whipped out the second pack she'd brought from the utility, and began to assemble a portable defibrillator.

'I'll shock him,' Alex said to her. 'Done it enough times in ER.'

'But not with a portable, I shouldn't think,' Kenzie said, not exactly pushing him away but making it very clear she was in charge.

'We've all trained on it—the senior staff,' Wayne explained, while doing chest compressions on the man. 'And once a year the RFDS have us do a simulation on their dummy during one of their clinic visits.'

Alex was only half listening, so he was surprised when Kenzie said, 'Clear,' and the man's body jolted as the shock went through it.

They all watched the screen, waiting for the miraculous wavy line that would tell them his heart was beating again.

Nothing.

'I'll do it again,' Kenzie said, and Alex, who'd taken over the chest compressions from Wayne, moved his hands.

And this time it worked, the heart lines appearing like magic on the screen.

'That's the plane,' Wayne said, apparently hearing a sound that was inaudible to Alex, although now he picked it up, and even saw the lights as the aircraft drew closer.

'We'll get them back to the strip. Wayne, you drive and Alex and I will stay in the back. Time check?'

For all that had happened it was surprising that it was only fifteen minutes since Wayne had applied the tourniquet. It would be safe to keep it there for an hour but it was essential for everyone concerned with the rescue to keep timing it.

Kenzie packed the defibrillator back in its small box with a feeling of relief that it had actually worked on a patient, but there was no time to gloat. The self-inflating mattresses were already filled with air, but they had to get both patients onto the lightweight stretchers and into the tray of the ute.

She glanced at Alex, now fitting a moon boot around the injured man's ankle, and wondered what he'd made of the whole adventure—well, hardly adventure, perhaps episode...

Now he and Wayne were slotting the two pieces of the stretcher together under their patient.

She returned to the young woman—Debbie—and with Steve's help got the other stretcher under her, for all she protested she could walk to the vehicle.

'No way,' Kenzie told her. 'There's every chance you've suffered a concussion. You were out to it when Steve found you.'

Once loaded up, they thanked Steve for his help and his call for assistance and, as he rode away to wherever he'd been going, Alex gave Kenzie a hand to scramble into the tray of the ute, where she settled beside the young man.

The plane had rolled to a stop and the steps were down by the time Wayne pulled up beside it. One of the nurses came down first, then Bill, one of their regular doctors, who helped Kenzie down from her perch and gave her a big hug.

'And you're the doctor chap who's married our Kenzie,' he said to Alex when Kenzie introduced them. 'I don't suppose you're looking for a job?'

Alex smiled at the suggestion, while Kenzie tried to imagine how different tonight's emergency situation had been, compared to the A and E department where he worked.

But all A and Es had their share of drama and excitement so maybe it had just been second nature to him...

Though he did go up into the plane.

Wanting to see his patients comfortably installed, or wanting to see the fit-out?

'Fantastic, isn't it?' he said, as he reached the ground again. 'I've flown in emergency evac aircraft in other places, but this is so streamlined.'

'Has to be,' Bill said. 'We never know what to expect from one minute to the next.'

The engines revved behind them and Bill held out his hand.

'Nice meeting you,' he said, and climbed

back into the aircraft, bringing up the steps behind him.

The party at the big shed was winding down, although young people still danced and sang to the music now playing.

'Dad must have gone to bed,' Kenzie said to Alex, nodding towards the noise. 'They'd never play pop music with him around.'

'Not gone to bed but gone to get a vehicle to take you two back to the house. Wayne'll take the ute.'

Her father appeared out of the shadows, and they stood and watched the plane take off, before getting into one of the big four-wheel drives to head back to the house.

'It's like a big extended family,' Alex said, as he and Kenzie entered their bedroom. 'Even the flying doctor chap seemed to belong.'

'It *is* my family,' Kenzie said.

They showered and went to bed, reaching for each other, surer now of each other's bodies and how they fitted best. Slow, languorous lovemaking that left Kenzie all but asleep beside him.

But as she slept, he tried to consider the enormity of the place he'd seen only part of today, to consider the people—her family—any one of whom would skin him alive if he hurt her.

He smiled to himself. As if he could! The love he felt for her was unlike anything he'd ever experienced.

And it was *that* that had him lying awake by her side. Staring out through the French doors, glimpses of the magic sky visible through the shrubs.

Could he really take her away from this dry, red-brown land she loved? From the people who loved her?

And how could their children learn enough from their grandfather and the men and women around him, if they were only here a couple of months a year?

Could his children swing from trees or climb hay bales, or roar around on little dirt bikes—they'd been doing that as well—back in Edinburgh?

There was a freedom in this place, and magic too, and, yes, he knew an enormous amount of work and organisation must go into it to make it run smoothly, yet Kenzie knew she could take over from her father, and would expect her children—or one of them at least—to want to do the same from her.

And beyond that was the totally surreal experience of the accident they'd attended. Wayne and Kenzie heading out to help some strangers, so organised they'd even had a professional tourniquet. He wanted—needed, he rather thought—to learn more about their first-aid equipment, while seeing the Royal Flying Doctor Service in action had stirred something in his gut.

Was there a job there for the taking?

'It isn't all skinny-dipping and beer and barbecues,' Kenzie told him when he tried to broach something of what he felt the next morning.

He was already up when she awoke, and had walked around the buildings close to the house. He'd had a cup of tea in the kitchen with Maggie, and had brought a tray to Kenzie in their bedroom, sitting on the bed while she drank it.

'I do realise that,' he said, 'but, anyway, that will be your job. But I wonder, if we switched, lived here and went to Scotland for holidays? Could you teach me to fly?'

'A small plane like we have here or the chopper, yes. You'd need proper professional lessons before getting your licence. Why?'

'Because I think I still have to be a doctor, and Tom—one of the pilots who flew me here—was talking about the Flying Doctor service, then last night I saw it all in action—not just you and Wayne as professional as any paramedics, but the plane coming in—it's like a special kind of magic, the way things happen out here in the middle of nowhere, to use your words.'

He smiled and bent to kiss her on the lips, tasting honey from the hives they'd seen yesterday, and Kenzie, his beautiful, magical wife…

She kissed him back then returned to his question—the teach me to fly one.

'You don't need to be able to fly to be a flying doctor. They have pilots.'

'I do know that,' he said. 'But if I could fly, I could get back here from Darwin much faster than driving when I have my days off.'

He paused, then added, 'Do you think that would work? Maybe an apartment in Darwin where we could both live when I'm on duty. Some of the time, anyway.'

She moved the tray from her legs and sat up very straight.

'Are you saying we'd live here? You'd move here? Alex, it's stinking hot and dry and dusty except in the wet when it buckets down without stopping the heat, and everything grows mould. And there's nothing here—no theatre, no movies, no lovely restaurants to dine in. It's about as far from beautiful, civilised Edinburgh as you could get. And you'd want to *live* here?'

He smiled at her.

'You'd like to, so why wouldn't I?' he said. 'And think of the children—the freedom they'd have. Not having to put on wellingtons and raincoats every time they go outside—even in summer a lot of the time.'

He paused, trying to find the words.

'I saw those children last night, Kenzie, and thought every child deserved a taste of what they've got.'

'Oh, Alex, do you really mean it?'

Kenzie's doubt and disbelief was written on her face.

'It's barely been two days. How can you tell you'd like it? You'd be bored, and you hate boredom.'

'I won't be bored if I'm working, and I'm assuming after some years here I might have learned enough to be useful to either your father or you. I like the way your father's thinking about calm cattle and I think drones could probably do the work your helicopters do now in spotting cattle for muster. Drones are silent.'

Kenzie shook her head.

'He's got one drone, but is only just learning how to fly it. Maybe a drone licence before your pilot's. I can ferry you around until you get that!'

'So it sounds doable?' he asked, suddenly aware of the huge change to his life he was considering.

'More than doable, *and* wonderful!' she said, giving him a hug. 'But we need to do a fair bit of homework about it all. You've got responsibilities back in Scotland—your grandmother's estate for one.'

'That's been managed by the same family for almost as long as the Monroes have owned it. I can keep in touch via the internet, and if we visit once a year—maybe during your wet—I can check all is well.'

'You really think so?' She looked at him, doubt in her lovely eyes, as if fearing this might not be quite real.

And he heard the doubt when she said, 'We still need time to think it through. It has to work as smoothly as possible or you might resent making the decision.'

'Resent the decision to live with you in the place you love? I doubt that very much,' he said, and kissed her, glad she'd removed the tray from the bed when the kiss turned into something more intimate.

EPILOGUE

'I THOUGHT MONROES didn't do emotion,' Kenzie said softly as Alex, cradling his newborn son, kissed her, hands trembling and tears streaking his cheeks.

She wiped the tears away with the edge of the sheet, and kissed the dark-haired head of her infant.

'Only sometimes,' he said, reluctantly settling the baby back in her arms.

He was in the crisp white shirt that was the uniform of the RFDS doctors, and had flown in from a road accident just in time to be with Kenzie for the birth.

'So, Andrew Monroe Steele, are we happy to go with that?' he said to her, his hand on her shoulder, needing to touch her.

She smiled at him.

'Too much if we add McLeod?' she said, smiling at him.

'Getting to be a bit of a mouthful,' he said, but he *was* pleased.

'Then we drop the Steele,' she said. 'He doesn't need it, he'll know he's a Steele.'

'Andrew Monroe McLeod! I like it.'

She reached out her free hand to cup his cheek.

'So do I!' she said. 'Everything about it! Especially the Monroe because your grandmother brought us together, and the McLeod, because that is you.'

He leant in carefully so as not to disturb Andrew, and kissed her on the lips, seeing the colour rise in her cheeks and happiness shining in her beautiful blue eyes.

* * * * *

LET'S TALK

For exclusive extracts, competitions and special offers, find us online:

 facebook.com/millsandboon

⊙ @millsandboonuk

🐦 @millsandboon

Or get in touch on 0844 844 1351*

For all the latest titles coming soon, visit millsandboon.co.uk/nextmonth